CU00704203

THE THREE MISTRESSES AND THE

AROUSAL ARMY

★ FEMDOM BOOT CAMP SERIES ★

★ BOOK 1 ★

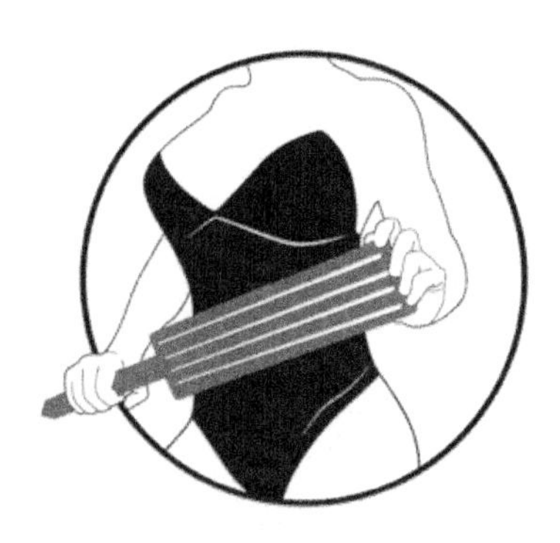

MILEY COYOTE

This is a fictional work. All names, characters, businesses, places, events and incidents in this book are either the product of the author's imagination or used in a fictitious manner. Any resemblance to actual persons, living or dead, or actual events is purely coincidental.

Table of Contents

1: Why Did I Answer That Ad? 5

2: I Want YOU for the Arousal Army 17

3: The Loincloth Lineup 38

3: Marches and Formations 83

4: Standing at Attention 103

5: Good Night and Sweet Dreams 117

6: Locked in a Chastity Cage 130

7: The Youngest New Recruit 142

8: Stamina 170

9: Inspiring Speech by Mistresses 187

10: Boot Licking 201

11: Public Funishment 214

12: The One Who Tries to Come Back 230

13: sissy Charlene's Observations 241

1: Why Did I Answer That Ad?

Why on earth did I think it would be a good idea to come all the way to Denver to compete with over 100 loincloth-clad men for the opportunity to serve not one—but three—powerful Mistresses? Why did I answer that ad? I notice my thoughts racing as I check out the scene surrounding me, Theodore Thompson, a New Recruit fighting for a chance to be a submissive servant and plaything to three gorgeous Mistresses at the 10th annual Arousal Army Femdom Boot Camp.

The dominatrixes are known as Mistress Insomnia, Mistress Doom, and Mistress Intrigue, and the practically naked New Recruits surrounding me are all waiting eagerly to see the ladies for the first time. I am standing in a group of at least 100 nearly nude men wearing only suede loincloths. As soon as the men arrived, the Mistresses and their team of sissies made us strip down, shave, and put ourselves into male chastity devices so that we would be on our best behavior.

We are all lined up on yard lines on the field at Mile

High Stadium in Denver, Colorado. It's a bit windy and chilly today, and the icy breeze blows my suede loincloth. I feel awkward, exposed, and a little nauseated. Not only am I nervous to meet the dommes, but I had a rough flight.

For the duration of Femdom Boot Camp, when I am training here at Mile High stadium, I am only allowed to wear this tan suede loincloth (which barely covers a thing!) and the cock cage underneath. The stainless-steel device features multiple welded rings that encircle my penis and lock into a ring around my balls. When I am wearing it, I can't have a full erection or pleasure myself. The male chastity cage is definitely a bit uncomfortable, especially because the stainless steel is chilly against my member. As the breeze continues to blow and lift our loincloths, I notice some of the men's members look a little cold and shrunken in their chastity devices.

Maybe that'll give me a better chance? I think hopefully. I'm here competing for an opportunity to serve not just one, but three powerful Mistresses, so I'll take any advantage I can get! Honestly, I am not sure how I'll measure up to the other New Recruits. *What do they all do for a living?* I wonder. I know the $120,000 application fee likely weeded out quite a few candidates.

I flew to Denver from a suburb of New York City, and I paid over $300,000 in tribute for the honor of being a contender to serve three strong Mistresses at the Arousal Army Femdom Boot Camp. I have already dropped $420,000 just to have a chance to be in the presence of these Mistresses, and they can reject me at any moment. I've never felt so vulnerable and insignificant before.

In my normal life, I'm a 24-year-old hedge fund manager on Wall Street, so I'm richer than most guys my age. But here, I know all the New Recruits have paid at least $420,000 just to be in the ladies' presence for Femdom Boot Camp, so I'm not so sure how much my wealth will make me stand out. What's more apparent here is my beer belly and pale white skin that show my lifestyle; I'll be the first to admit I drink too much, rarely work out, and never leave the office or spend time outdoors.

I'm starting to worry I might not make the cut, after everything I've sacrificed to be here. My penis feels shriveled in its cold steel cage, too. I've never done anything like this before, but I've definitely fantasized about being dominated, tied up, and forced to serve a strong and powerful woman. So, when I saw the ad for Femdom Boot Camp in *Kinky Times,* I jumped at the chance to attend to three dominatrixes!

My name is Theodore Thompson, and I'm a recent New York University graduate with a finance degree. I work long hours on Wall Street and reap great financial rewards. In my everyday life, I have plenty of money, and therefore plenty of female attention. Still, I've been feeling a strange sense of ennui, a boredom that haunts me during my day-to-day activities. I feel like I want…something more.

I am hoping that surrendering in complete submission to these three fierce dominatrixes will satisfy my deeper desires, but I do feel vaguely uncomfortable and self-conscious being practically naked around so many strange men. I'm not totally sure how to act in this bizarre new world, where many of the power dynamics I've been raised with are totally reversed. Here, it's clear the women—and their costumed, made up, and perfumed sissy slaves—are running the show, and not the rugged, masculine New Recruits.

The other New Recruits standing around me range in age from men who look like they are barely 18 to men who look like they were born in 1918; there are a variety of body shapes and sizes also. Some men are extremely buff and look like they spend hours at the gym; others look more like they spend hours lying on the couch and watching Netflix while eating popcorn. My body shape is definitely closer to the latter than the former.

The crowd of men and I are standing at alert and

facing a stage that has been set up in the middle of Mile High Stadium in Denver, Colorado. Suddenly, I hear the voice of a sissy shout, "Woo hoo, boys, here they come!" I notice the posture of every New Recruit straightens up, as the men stand at attention and try to make their best first impression.

Moments later, a crew of six men wearing ball gags and black leather loincloths enter the stadium with their eyes lowered. They all have bulging muscles and completely shaved heads. They are carrying Mistress Doom, Mistress Intrigue, and Mistress Insomnia on a type of carriage box on their shoulders. I strain to get my first glimpse of the latex and leather-clad goddesses.

Once the crew arrives at the stage, the bare-chested men set the transport box down and open the door for the three Mistresses to disembark. It is dazzling to see the women stand atop the stage. They are wearing full-body catsuits, and each one has her own megaphone. The megaphones seem to be decorated with rhinestones that sparkle.

Quinn, my fraternity brother from New York University, notices me staring at the megaphones. "You know, that guy with the earrings told me those aren't rhinestones. They're real diamonds," he says.

I look at him with awe. "Really?"

"Yeah, man. Many of their submissives are extremely wealthy, and they love to pay tribute to and pamper their Mistresses."

I am starting to feel insecure, not only about my pasty white flesh, protruding potbelly, and wild chest hairs, but about my income and career ranking. I can't help but wonder how I'll stack up. Some of these dudes are young and ripped! I notice a balding older man and think, *at least I still have all my hair!*

Normally working on Wall Street seems like a pretty big deal, and quite a few ladies have dropped their panties after I spent a night wining and dining them. But here, being a successful hedge fund manager doesn't differentiate me at all. Sadly, I think, *the thing they'll notice most is my pale works-inside-all-day furry chest and my chubby gut.*

The Mistresses, on the other hand, are gorgeous. Mistress Insomnia has mid-length black hair with bangs. Her stylish hair has been cut in a sharp angle that accentuates her high cheekbones. Her dark locks match her full-body black leather catsuit, and her kohl-lined eyes emanate a strong seductive energy. I can't help but wonder how it would feel to rub the leather bodysuit and the Mistress inside of it.

Mistress Insomnia is brandishing a leather riding crop with a rainbow-colored handle. I imagine her using it on me and notice I am becoming quite aroused from the mere thought of it... My cock chafes against the cage as my penis grows harder. It's difficult not to be turned on. Mistress Insomnia appears quite tall, almost like a giant. Her legs look even longer because of her platform patent leather boots. The heel looks to be at least six inches tall, with a two-inch platform…

Mistress Insomnia is quite curvy, with an hourglass figure. I notice her full booty and breasts jiggle when she walks. I think that Mistress Insomnia somewhat resembles Bettie Page, the pinup model, but she is taller, and she does not exude the same playful, girlish energy. She appears to be quite stern. I feel I might turn to ice just from receiving Mistress Insomnia's cold, steely gaze. Her eyes are ice blue, and her skin is pale white. *She probably doesn't get out in the sun much because she's always down in her dungeon,* I think.

I heard that, a female voice fills my mind, as a haunting image of Mistress Insomnia's eyes fills my thoughts. *What the heck is that about?* I think, unconsciously rubbing my third eye in the middle of my forehead. I glance quickly up at the next Mistress. I am trying to keep my eyes downcast, to appear calm and submissive to the trio of dominatrixes, but my curiosity keeps getting the best of me, so I steal glances of the beautiful women every chance I get.

Mistress Intrigue is quite slender, and extraordinarily tall. Born in Japan, she won a contest as a teenager and received a modeling contract that launched her career in New York and on international runways. I think she looks elegant in her skintight black latex catsuit. Her bodysuit features a silver zipper that wraps around her crotch and up to her lower back so that she could unzip the entire lower part of the suit. She has long, straight black hair and a surprisingly innocent-looking face, with wide eyes well-accentuated with thick black eyeliner.

Mistress Intrigue lets out a full-bellied laugh. The cackle sounds sadistic, and I wonder if she might be not quite as angelic as she first appears. She has tiny titties, and I enjoy imagining myself cupping one breast while suckling the other. I feel my dick growing hard and pulling against the cold steel chastity cage I'd been fitted with earlier. It feels awkward having this contraption attached to my manhood, but it is worth it to have the opportunity to explore my call to submission.

This is better than any fantasy I've ever imagined. The sight of these dominant women is sending me deep into the subspace, and they haven't even spoken yet! I've never felt so clear-headed and safe in my life. The feeling is amazing, but difficult to describe. It almost feels like a euphoric drug, but it's even better and stronger than any substance I've ever tried.

Mistress Intrigue holds tightly to a thick black flogger with dozens of leather strips about 18 inches long and two inches wide hanging down. Her hot pink claw-shaped nails practically glow against the black leather grip of the flogger. She snaps the tool hard and fast against her knee-high stiletto patent leather boots, and my dick grows harder as I listen to the sound. My suede loincloth rises as my hard dick swells inside the cage and lifts the front flap. I feel an uncomfortable sensation as my penis meets the cold steel of the cage. I think I hear a few New Recruits snickering at me.

"Ahem," Mistress Doom clears her throat. Standing at a petite 5'3", Mistress Doom seems almost miniature next to the giantesses. Mistress Doom is a seductive African-American woman with a shaved head and piercing green eyes. Her extremely short hair is dyed the color of marigolds and looks lovely contrasting with her dark skin. She is very curvaceous and is clad from head to toe in a black leather catsuit. Her bodysuit features flaps over the breasts and crotch. I think her ebony skin is so beautiful. I find myself wishing I could open the flaps to touch and feel her soft rolling curves underneath the catsuit.

Then, out of nowhere, I see a vivid flash of some sort of erotic kiss between me and the three Mistresses in my mind's eye. *What the heck?* I think. A terrible sharp pain passes through my nether regions while a sinister-sounding cackle echoes in my mind. *Is that Mistress Intrigue? Can she read my thoughts?*

"Ouch!" I scream. I hear another cackle from my right. Mistress Intrigue has crept up near me and flogged my erect penis without my noticing. Her cackle had not been merely a thought after all.

"Ouch?" she asks, and raises an eyebrow. "Try again, slave."

"I mean, thank you, Mistress."

"That's better. Now go take a cold shower and come back when you've got that disgusting man meat under control, New Recruit."

"Not so quick," Mistress Doom says as she steps up to my left.

Her leather boots come up to her knees and have laces down the front. She is brandishing a wooden paddle with hearts cut out of it. She wraps her fingers around the paddle, and her golden nails sparkle in the light. They are also filed into points, like cat's claws.

I take in her full bust and can't help but ogle Mistress Doom's ample cleavage, which is pouring out of her tightly zipped catsuit. I hope she's distracted enough that she won't notice my lustful gaze.

Out of nowhere, Quinn whispers in my ear, "They're pretty hot, huh?" I still am not used to seeing my old college buddy at the Femdom Boot Camp. I was in the same fraternity with Quinn at NYU, but I had no idea the dude was into BDSM. Now, he's been placed on the yard line next to me, so it looks like we'll be seeing a lot more of each other. I can't help but check him out. The dude looks like a

Greek Adonis with curly dark blonde hair and great washboard abs. Yet again, my penis pulls at its chastity cage. I wince in pain as the cold metal wraps around my engorged member, which quickly deflates at the sensation.

I hear a woman roar: "Submissives are to be seen and not heard!" Mistress Insomnia shouts into her bejeweled megaphone from the stage. I glance up and see the tall giantess crack the riding crop against her leather gloved hand. *If only that had been against my booty,* I fantasize for a moment what that might feel like.

"That means YOU!" she bellows loudly and hits the riding crop hard several times against her black glove. I hear the loud "thwat" it makes as leather hits leather. At that moment, the head of every New Recruit pivots to see who has gotten her attention. I nearly wet my loincloth when I see she is looking right at me and Quinn with her ice blue eyes.

I have to force myself not to bite my fingernails or scratch myself, both nervous tics I've had since childhood. Instead, I stand really still and hope I'm not in trouble. Although, I think, being in trouble might not be so bad if that means...punishment. Maybe I'd get a chance to experience being at the receiving end of that riding crop if the stars aligned. I almost come just imagining it, and I feel my experience of subspace deepen. Being out here, caged and almost naked, ordered around by three dommes, is a sweet torture and a sweet bliss. I am in it to win it at this point, and I want more. In fact, I want to be with all three of the Mistresses!

Mistress Doom, who is still right next to me, clears her throat. "This is total and complete insubordination," she says with a lilting Southern drawl. "You two have already been such bad boys. Both of you, bend over, NOW!" she commands. Quinn and I both drop our torsos down and stick out our rear ends. The curvy, petite dominatrix approaches us from behind. First, Mistress Doom puts her hand on Quinn's back, then thump! She uses her wooden paddle and delivers a powerful blow to Quinn's round, squeezable butt. I hear him whimper a bit and see him jump forward from the force. His rear has turned red, in the shape of the heart on the paddle.

"Ouch!" he screams suddenly. Mistress Intrigue has crept up on his other side and is grabbing his ear. "You forgot the ending remarks, newbie," she growls, and flips her long hair over her shoulder. Mistress Intrigue taps the toe of her stiletto boots impatiently on the ground. "Say, 'Thank you, Mistress' to appreciate the hard work of discipline you just made Mistress Doom do."

"T-t-thank you, Mistress," Quinn stutters. His voice sounds different—more meek or feminine somehow.

This is not the Quinn I'd known during college. I hadn't tapped into this part of myself then yet either, though. I wonder when Quinn realized he is into being dominated…

Now, bent over here in my loincloth, trying to be a good boy for this sexy full-figured goddess, I am grateful Quinn went first so I can follow his example. I press my butt out and wait… For a few moments, Mistress Doom pretends she is about to deliver a blow, but never does. Each time I jump in anticipation, and the three Mistresses laugh as they watch my nervousness increase. Finally, Mistress Doom spanks my heinie hard with the wooden paddle. I want to rub the stinging area but resist. I don't want to upset Mistress Doom. She may be short, but she is definitely strong and powerful.

"Thank you, Mistress," I say humbly.

"Good boy," she says. The words are like music to my ears. I feel the sweet submissive part deep inside of me fill up with her encouraging words. It feels so good to know I have pleased her. Little do I know that feeling won't last, and that I'll end up in the dog house mere hours later. But I'm getting a bit ahead of myself. Let me go back and start at the very beginning…

2: I Want YOU for the Arousal Army

Even though at age 24, I am already a respected and successful Wall Street broker, I have secretly longed for full submission to a dominatrix for years. When I was younger, I noticed I was attracted to "bitchy" girls who did not tolerate disrespect, but I always ended up going out with sweet, good girls that I thought were socially acceptable. Part of that had to do with my adoptive parents. They are kind people who happen to be well-connected in the New York financial world. Still, their strict Catholic worldview somewhat limits their perspective, in my opinion.

As a young man, I felt I had to live an especially upright and moral life so that I could impress them and continue to play a part in their lives. Once I left home and went to college, though, I started to question the tenets of religion, and their grip on my sense of morality started to fade. But even now, when I visit home, I do my best to keep up appearances for them. Part of that involves having a so-called "normal" (heterosexual, marriage-based) relationship.

When I was in college at New York University, I had a girlfriend who wanted to get married so badly that she would do anything to please me. She would cook for me, give me massages, and even tidy up my apartment. She was sweet and kind; there was nothing wrong with her, but the sweeter she was, and the more placating she became, the less aroused by her I felt. So, I ended the relationship with the classic line, "It's not you. It's me." I didn't know how to explain my true desires, much less elicit them from such a compliant and pampering woman.

After the breakup, I was still too scared to admit my deeper submissive yearnings to a real-life woman. I wasn't sure how to approach it, and aside from checking out dominatrixes on Fetlife occasionally after work, I didn't take any action.

After a few months of this, I decided I could at least explore my interests a little, so I subscribed to *Kinky Folks* magazine. This periodical features sexy bondage photos, sissies held in chastity, and so much more. I look forward to it every month as a break from my humdrum workaholic existence.

I was sitting on the couch and reading my monthly copy of *Kinky Folks* magazine when I saw the ad for the Arousal Army recruitment event. The full-page advertisement featured a sexy woman with dark hair and bangs wearing a skintight leather catsuit and an

Uncle Sam-style top hat (re-done in black, red, gray, and white stripes). She was smiling beguilingly and pointing toward the viewer. Her hand was cased alluringly in a silk glove.

As soon as I saw the sexy woman's mysterious image, I undid my trouser button and unzipped my pants. I slid my hand down to my crotch and into my silk boxers. I loved the feeling of silk against my skin, and I especially liked experimenting with colors by purchasing unique boxers. I wished I could wear a wider variety of colors and styles, but as a Wall Street man, I felt boxed into the traditional suit and tie. Wearing fun underwear gave me a slight feeling of freedom, and no one had to know what was going on under my trousers.

I pulled my now-erect cock through the hole in my shorts and started pumping it hard with my hand. My eyes rolled back into my head as waves of pleasure filled my body. I let out a soft moan and glanced at the woman's image in the ad again. I stared into her eyes as I massaged my pre-cum into the tip of my dick. Her eyes, boldly lined with onyx cat eye eyeliner, caught mine, and in an instant, I came all over the copy of *Kinky Times*.

I rested for a moment with my hand on my belly, enjoying the pleasure pulsing throughout my body and the calm, relaxed sensation I felt. I glanced over at the magazine and wiped off a bit of semen that had fallen on the cheek of the intoxicating photo.

Once I'd cleaned my jizz off the cover of *Kinky Times,* I suddenly noticed a message underneath the photo: "I want YOU for the Arousal Army." My curiosity was piqued. What was the Arousal Army, and who was this woman? Should I sign up for it, whatever it was? *After all, the fact I came on her face is probably a sign,* I thought.

After a bit of a rest, I picked up the ad again and squinted at the small print. It said:

"New Recruits will go through strict training at Femdom Boot Camp, hosted at Mile High Stadium in Denver, Colorado.

Full application with background check and fee required for attendance.

See https://www.patreon.com/mileycoyote for more information."

At first, I laughed at the ad. Feeling a bit awkward, I also started biting my nails and scratching my ear. Although I usually managed to hide it, I am somewhat shy and still have some nervous tics from childhood.

Who would go for that ad? I thought. *It sounds pretty hardcore.* I imagined some pathetic old hairy dude with no sex life who had to pay for some intrigue might be willing to reply. But surely a young, successful man like myself wouldn't need to respond to such an ad to enhance my love life, right? Was there even a potential for love at the Femdom Boot Camp, or would I be getting myself in over my head by submitting to three cruel, sadistic dominatrixes?

I put the idea aside, until I found myself jacking off to the picture nearly daily. The Mistress's image had gotten warped because I'd come on her face so many times during my daily masturbation session. I knew I should probably be edging, and possibly, saving my hardness for her, but I craved the release of an orgasm and never tried to contain my sexual drive on my own. I loved to hope and dream it was possible to attain a sense of complete submission under the leadership of a dominant woman, but I was also terrified of what might unfold.

I finally decided to build up my courage and just go for it. I took my monthly trip to the gym and got pumped, and after a nice shower and some time spent listening to my favorite jazz music, I felt ready to apply. I was nervous my adoptive mom or dad or extended relatives might find out, but I told myself to go ahead anyway. *You're a grown up now,* I thought, *so stop caring what other people think and just go for your dreams!*

Soon my dreams would be filled with nothing but her... It was such sweet torture. I would often wonder if I'd made the right choice, and her eyes, and her voice, would always bring me back to kneel at her boots. Once I actually arrived in Colorado, I learned the photo had been of Mistress Insomnia. She'd be my Mistress—or rather, I'd be her pet…at least I secretly hoped so. I wasn't sure who I could to talk to about my yearnings, so I began to keep a daily journal.

Day 1 - The Application

I was intoxicated by a woman's eyes in an ad and decided to apply to be a New Recruit in the Arousal Army. Am I insane? I can't sleep because I can't stop thinking of her.... And wishing she were flogging me while clad head to toe in latex, or holding me in handcuffs, or possibly using me as her sex slave...

Theodore T.

The diary entry trailed off as I settled in for the night, rubbing my hard cock and imagining the mysterious woman's full form… I ejaculated on the page and then drifted off to sleep.

The application was not a simple task. Each individual had to submit a set of photos (clothed in a gentleman's suit, flexing while wearing underwear, and fully nude) with poses from the front, side, and behind (while bending over). I chose to take mine using the auto-timer feature on my phone because I could not fathom letting anyone else see me nude, much less know I was submitting the application. I'd always been pretty shy about my body. I was the dude who wore a T-shirt to the pool party most of my life. I never in my wildest dreams imagined I'd be taking erotic self-portraits to send to three mystery Mistresses.

The Arousal Army application also required clean recent STD test results and a hefty application fee ($120,000). Each potential New Recruit in the Arousal Army went through a professional background check that included credit scores and criminal history.

The thorough 20-page application included standard questions such as age and address; it also addressed kinks, sexual interests, BDSM experience, and soft and hard limits. I was pleasantly surprised to see it ended with some introspective self-awareness and life purpose questions. I already knew that for me submission should be my way of life, and I felt some sense of spiritual depth underneath my desire. I was seeking out this experience not just for transitory sense pleasure, but also to help me fill this void deep within, in the part of me that longed to submit to the divine feminine power.

Arousal Army: New Recruit Application
Name: *Theodore Thompson*

Please check all that interest you:

[X] Rope Bondage
[X] Suspension
[X] Cuffs, Gags, Blindfolds
[X] Spanking with Floggers, Paddles, and Canes
[ ] Bruises/Marks
[X] Hot/Cold Sensation Play
[X] D/s role play scenarios
[X] Submissive slave lifestyle
[X] Humiliation and degradation
[ ] Orgasm control and denial
[?] Pet play
[!!] Chastity cage
[X] Dressing up, latex, lace, leather, make up, heels

For weeks, I felt nervous every day when I checked the mail and my e-mail. I wasn't sure how or if the Mistresses would contact me if I was accepted into the Arousal Army. Every time my phone rang or a text message arrived, I jumped. I almost wet my pants, I was so nervous waiting to hear back from the dominatrixes. Would I be a New Recruit? And would anyone else be crazy enough to apply?

After 37 days (I knew because I'd notched the count into my bedpost each night), a golden envelope with elegant black calligraphy arrived addressed to Mr. Theodore Thompson. I thought I had been excited to get into NYU, but that acceptance letter had nothing on this one! I could feel my penis getting hard just holding the envelope, and I hadn't even opened it yet.

For a moment I let myself imagine my hot blonde neighbor Jane walking by, undoing my belt, and lowering my pants so she could lick and suck my cock. I often saw her when I got my mail. Lost in my reverie, I felt my hand creeping over my belly toward my belt, until a noise from behind startled me.

"What's that nifty letter got inside?" asked Jane, the blonde from next door. Jane was married to Brady and, at least on the surface of things, they appeared to be your typical suburban couple. Brady was a brawny man who did construction and repairs at home in his free time, when he wasn't running his construction firm.

Jane pursed her red lipsticked lips and winked at me, batting her eyelashes flirtatiously. She was wearing a professional-looking form-fitting dark blue pencil skirt that hugged her curves. I noticed it had a slight slit in the back and that she was wearing old-fashioned hosiery with a seam up the back. She had on a sheer white polka dot button-up blouse over a silk tank. I could barely see the outline of her white bra through the top. The petite woman finished the look with classic navy pumps with a stiletto heel. I wasn't sure if I was hallucinating or still lost in my sexual fantasy from earlier. I felt nervous holding that letter with Jane looking at me like that.

"N-n-n-nothing," I stated.

"Yeah, right! You're blushing," Jane squealed. "You expect me to buy that?" She playfully punched me on the shoulder. I could've sworn she then stuck out her chest and ass to pose for my view.

"Uh..." I was speechless.

"Fine, keep your secret golden letter, Theodore," Jane said and swiveled around on her stiletto heels. Her coarse navy pencil skirt highlighted her tight ass, and the sheer button up blouse revealed her fine physique and her tan. Her blonde hair was curled and pinned up neatly in a twist that revealed her cute neck.

My eyes took in her voluptuous figure as she walked away. That ass... I felt my hand unconsciously seeking out my hard cock yet again, but I stopped myself. *Dude, you're still in public!* I thought, a bit frantically.

Was she flirting with me? I honestly wasn't too sure. I'd always been a bit socially awkward. All I knew for sure was that I wanted to open the letter now, and then masturbate to the *Kinky Times* ad again before calling it a night…

I clasped the gilded letter between my hands and headed up the steps to my light blue two-story colonial house. After graduating with my degree in finance from the New York University Stern School of Business, I tried living in an apartment in Manhattan with a college friend. It had been an expensive, confining nightmare. I longed for more relaxation, and sought peace and quiet in the New Jersey suburbs. After a year of suffering in the fast-paced and crowded city (and with a roommate nonetheless!), I decided to purchase an actual house with a yard in a suburban neighborhood in Ridgefield Park, NJ.

It was a bachelor pad for now, but I hoped to find the right partner and have kids…someday. I'd done a bit of reading on female-led relationships and secretly hoped I would meet a strong, powerful woman who could lead me to complete submission through our partnership. I felt foolish for thinking it, but I hoped that perhaps whatever was in this golden envelope would be an answer to my prayers.

I took a deep breath and, hands shaking, opened the envelope to reveal a creamy white letter on high-quality paper folded up inside. I pulled the letter from its envelope and unfolded it.

"Ouch!" I exclaimed as I got a paper cut from the

letter's edge. A drop of blood fell on the note and pooled around an ornate gold embossed logo that said Arousal Army Femdom Boot Camp. The bright red drop saturated the paper and left a pool of blood covering the word Femdom. I blinked and shrugged. *Oh well,* I thought. *What does this say anyway?* I hoped it was good news. Surely they wouldn't send such a fancy letter just to reject me, would they?

Arousal Army Femdom Boot Camp

Theodore Thompson
3212 Chicadee Lane
Ridgefield Park, NJ 07660

Dearest Theodore,

Mistress Insomnia, Mistress Intrigue, and Mistress Doom are pleased to cordially invite you to audition as a New Recruit at this year's Arousal Army Femdom Boot Camp training program, where only the strongest—and most submissive—survive.

Our rigorous training will stretch you to your physical, emotional, mental, and spiritual limits. At the end, you'll wish we just wanted your money. Don't get us wrong; we love your tributes. But what we really want is you—namely, to own you: body, mind, heart, and soul.

If you think you have what it takes, pack your bags for our 6-month program, meeting at Mile High Stadium in

Denver, Colorado. Plan for all weather; training begins in May and wraps up in October.

Be sure to pack:

(1) Formal suit and tie with shoes
(2) Your finest boxers, thongs, and briefs
(3) Any of your favorite toys or kinky tools
(4) Toiletries and personal items
(5) Tribute for three Mistresses
[Amazon list available here.]

The Arousal Army Femdom Boot Camp is a demanding training camp; do not attend if you have any doubts, because only those with full commitment will manage to make it through successfully.

If you think you're up to the challenge, get ready for the experience of a lifetime! If you choose to accept the mission, book a one-way flight to arrive in Denver on May 1. Not every potential New Recruit will last through the entire Boot Camp, so be prepared to book your return flight once you are relieved of duty to the Mistresses.

Remember, submissives are to be seen and not heard!

Submit your travel itinerary at the address listed on the envelope so we can arrange your transportation and lodging on arrival.

★

Congratulations, and welcome to the next chapter of your life!

You belong to us,

Mistress Insomnia
Mistress Doom
Mistress Intrigue

Wow, I thought, my hand still gripping the letter. I noticed I'd gotten an erection again just from reading it. I'd been single for years, but I occasionally found someone to help me find some sexual release without forming a formal relationship. My mind flashed to the mental image of that tight wool pencil skirt plastered to my neighbor Jane's curvy ass. I moved my hand down and pulled out my cock again. As I re-read the letter, I stroked and tugged on my member, which had started to pulsate with pleasure.

Who were these Mistresses? I thought. I was amazed there were three of them. I threw myself down on the leather couch in my parlor and started frantically masturbating. My head fell back over the arm of the couch, and my eyes rolled back into my head as I thrust my hips and pumped my cock with my tightly closed hand. With a slight moan, I spit in my hand

and used the moistness to lubricate my steady stroking motion.

As I pleasured myself, I imagined the Mistresses. In my mind, they all wore head-to-toe shiny latex suits that were skintight, and they were all smoking hot. Mistress Insomnia came and wrapped a blindfold over my eyes. I imagined her saying, "You're such a good boy, Theodore. So well-behaved…" and then heard the others chime in.

"I disagree. I think this boy is quite naughty," I heard a husky voice say.

"Do you think he needs to be punished?" A third, higher-pitched and singsong voice chimed in.

"Definitely!" The woman with the deeper voice laughed throatily and told me to bend over. Still wearing the blindfold, I felt her hands on my hips guide me to what felt like a bed. She pushed me gently on my back so that I bent forward, my chest resting on the soft mattress.

The other woman, without any warning, unzipped my pants and whisked them off of my body, then yanked my (embarrassingly threadbare) boxers down to my ankles. I heard the Mistresses giggle and felt a cool breeze blowing over my now-exposed balls and penis.

The part of me that loved to be humiliated was getting hornier by the minute, imagining these strong and powerful women laughing at my masculine pride and joy, my pecker. The more they laughed, the harder it got. And the harder it got, the more they laughed.

"That little clitty is so adorable!" squealed one of the Mistresses.

"How can you even see it without your glasses?" shouted another, which led to raucous laughter among the three.

All of a sudden, I felt a warm hand on my bare ass.

"Ooh, he's got a nice, toned ass," cooed one of the Mistresses. "He must work out."

"As a matter of fact, I do," I crowed, subconsciously thrusting my now-bursting member forward into the air. Truth is, I skipped the gym for a night at the bar most nights, but still... I wanted to see and touch the gorgeous women around me, but I was stuck in the blindfold.

I began noticing smells and sounds I had never been aware of before. It seemed they were burning some sort of heady incense. The aroma was familiar, but I couldn't quite place it. All of a sudden, I heard a cough, and another giggle, and another cough.

"Go ahead and pass that thing!" one of the women said. I realized I was smelling marijuana, and they were smoking a joint. It was all I could do not to pull off my blindfold and see them smoking. I loved to watch ladies smoking, especially if they were wearing red lipstick. My pumping grew faster and stronger as

I stroked my erect cock, imagining the three latex-clad Mistresses sucking in smoke and exhaling it slowly from their lips.

In my imagination, light glinted off their shiny latex suits, which emphasized their beautiful breasts. Then, in my fantasy, one of the women paddled me—hard. I jumped, and they giggled again. My ass totally stung. I loved the pain. I imagined them grabbing a flogger, then a riding crop, and punishing me for being so naughty. As they did, they laughed, teased, and giggled. The more they spanked and taunted, the harder I got. I felt like I was going to burst.

"Please, divine Mistresses, permission to come. Please!" I begged.

"No, boy!" the husky voice shouted as a paddle pommeled my exposed ass. Next, I felt a bare hand spank hard on my left cheek. Finally, one of the Mistresses grabbed a riding crop and tapped my butt, hard.

"Ohhh…" I moaned, and then came, right there on the couch.

When I stood up, I noticed a silhouette outside my window. The sun was setting and I couldn't make out who was there, but they seemed to be watching me through the slightly opened blinds.

I quickly zipped up my pants and ran to the door. Yanking it open, I shouted, "Who's there?"

"It's me," said Jane, my hot neighbor, using a sweet, singsong voice. "You know, if you can keep that letter a secret, I can keep a secret, too. Have you ever thought about…you know?"

I could not believe my ears. Was I still fantasizing, or was this actually happening?

"What do you mean, Jane?" I asked. "Would you like to come inside and clarify?" I wondered if she'd seen me jacking off, and I got even more aroused imagining that she had.

Even though I was definitely physically attracted to this woman, I still had a sense of ethics, instilled in me from my religious upbringing and enhanced as I pursued a minor in Philosophy at NYU. Jane had caught me at a time when I was extremely horny and eager for a fuck, but in the back of my mind, I considered Brady. Would it come back to haunt me if I moved forward? I decided to try to keep things innocent.

"I'd love to come inside," she said, "and I hope you can say the same about coming inside me!" She walked in and spanked my ass as she shut the door. I was still holding my pants together with my hands, but the fly was still totally unzipped. Jane reached for my hands, putting each one into her own, which made me drop my pants. My fat, girthy dick was hard again and popped out of my boxers at high alert.

"Oooh, I see you're excited to see me," Jane murmured, and knelt down in front of me. "That thing is huge! Let me see what you taste like. Is that OK?" She looked at me with big, open eyes. I noticed they were blue.

I nodded, startled.

"Uh, sure, Jane. Go for it."

She started sucking the tip of my cock and teasing her tongue over the surface. I moaned and pushed my dick deeper in her mouth. Part of me still wondered, *what about Brady?* I didn't really know the dude, but he seemed like an OK guy. I wondered if something was wrong in the marriage between Jane and Brady.

Then my primal brain shut off the musings, and I started pumping and thrusting uncontrollably. Jane had lowered her face over my cock and deep-throated me. She moaned as she gently held and stroked my balls. Her spit was dripping out of her mouth and had completely coated my cock.

"I want you inside me—NOW," Jane insisted.

"Uh..." I muttered. My brain was reeling. My body definitely wanted the same thing, but my heart feared being part of infidelity.

While I hemmed and hawed, Jane began seductively stripping in front of me. She undid her hair clip and shook out her long, blonde hair. Then she slowly unbuttoned her sheer white blouse, looking me right in the eyes the entire time. Jane revealed her voluptuous breasts resting in a delicate white lace bra.

She unzipped her pencil skirt and pulled it off, and I gasped when I saw her matching white lace thong. Jane was quite fit and shapely. Her eyes caught mine and seemed to penetrate past all resistance. Jane was still wearing thigh-high nude stockings with seams down the back and shiny navy-blue stiletto heels with a sharp point.

She continued to look me straight in the eye as she went and closed the blinds. Jane grabbed my hand and led me over the couch, where she bent over and pushed her ass out toward me. With one hand, she pulled her lace thong aside, and with the other, she massaged her own clit and then stuck two fingers inside her pussy. I noticed her wet whiteness start to drip from her hole.

"Take me, Theodore," she said. "I've seen you looking at me. I've seen you staring at my ass and my breasts. And trust me, that letter isn't the only package of yours that I've noticed," Jane said and winked. "I'm so wet and horny for you now."

I had one of those stereotypical moments where there's a devil on one shoulder and an angel on another. The devil, of course, said, "Fuck her hard and come inside of her, Theodore." The angel said, "Do not break up someone's marriage for a moment of lust. Use your higher consciousness and practice restraint."

I settled for the middle path. I pushed my hard cock deep into her wet pussy and pounded her hard while she moaned and fingered her clit. I could see our reflection in the big hallway mirror, and I loved seeing her gorgeous breasts swinging back and forth in her lace bra as I fucked her hard from behind.

"Fuck me harder," she squealed, and I obliged. The two of us continued moaning and groaning for about half an hour until I was ready to come.

"I'm ready to jizz," I said, and quickly pulled out, spraying my cum all over her asscrack and back. I had to be honest; she looked incredibly hot in this moment. "You are looking good, Jane. Do you want to use my shower before you go home?" I asked.

She put her hands in the pools of cum and rubbed it over her breasts, then licked her fingers to taste my juices. I noticed she was still dripping wet. As hot as she was, I was coming back to reality. *What had I done?* Even though I wasn't a practicing Catholic any more, the idea of my sinfulness filled me from the teachings I received in my youth. I felt a bit repulsed by myself now and very guilty. *Was this how I was trying to fill the emptiness inside?*

Fortunately, Jane took my lead and went to my

guest bathroom to take a shower, while I redid my pants and tried to get presentable again. I noticed the golden envelope on my table and smiled. Today had turned out to be more exciting than I'd expected, in every conceivable way! I decided not to worry about things for now.

Jane turned off the shower and re-dressed, then gave me a quick kiss on the cheek before she turned to leave. "Call me any time, stud," she laughed as she shut the door and headed to her house across the street.

3: The Loincloth Lineup

Although I was a bit nervous, I wasted no time in getting my travel agent to arrange my flight to Denver on May 1. I packed a tailored black suit from my favorite mom-and-pop suit shop in New York City, along with a crisp white designer button-up shirt and a green silk tie. I also included some tight Calvin Klein briefs and silk boxers, a wooden paddle, and a butt plug with a furry tail attached. I tried to pack plenty of layers and to be prepared for any weather. I brought my finest clothes, and I purchased some things new so I could make my best impression.

I brought tribute for the three Mistresses, who had an Amazon wish list. I purchased a leather flogger and nipple clips for Mistress Insomnia, a soothing aromatherapy bath set and silk scarf for Mistress Intrigue, and several brainy academic texts and a wooden paddle for Mistress Doom. I really hoped they would appreciate my gifts and worried I should have purchased more items to win their good graces. *Would I be good enough and able to please them?* I was feeling more and more nervous with every passing day.

May 1 arrived quickly. For the trip, I wore a well-tailored lavender button-up shirt with belted black trousers and polished black leather shoes. I had straightened and blown dry my brown hair, which was a little on the long side and hung to the top of my ears. I gelled it back so that it would stay in place during travel. I finished my look off with my favorite Rolex watch.

I was so excited to arrive at Femdom Boot Camp, but I was also afraid. I hoped my dreams of submitting to a powerful Mistress could come true. As a student of Zen, I was excited for the potential ego release I could obtain through total and complete submission, and as warm-blooded male, I was aroused by the idea of experiencing some kinky situations. But I feared I might be found lacking, unable to please the Mistresses, and rejected. I also feared I might be pushed to my physical, mental, and emotional limits, and I wasn't sure how I would handle the various situations that might arise.

Still, I had to try. To distract myself, I chatted with the woman seated next to me in business class and enjoyed a can of beer. One can became two cans, which became three cans, and then maybe four or more cans. The flight attendants kept whisking away cans and bringing more whenever I asked. I couldn't remember nor keep track of how many they brought.

I do remember the woman sitting next to me smiling when I told her I worked in finance.

"Oh, so you're one of those Wall Street bigwigs, huh?" she said, as she grabbed and massaged my bicep. She leaned forward a bit and squeezed her medium-sized breasts together so that I would notice her cleavage. She was hot, and I was getting a bit turned on. "What are you up to in Denver?"

"I'll be completing some training at Mile High Stadium," I said.

My seat mate took a sip of her dirty martini and said, "Mile High, huh? Are you a member of the mile-high club yet?" She looked me in the eye and winked.

I noticed I was sweating profusely, and I began wringing my hands as the woman moved her hand to my upper thigh and squeezed.

"Uh, no, I'm not a member," I stammered.

"You want to be?" She winked and took another sip of her martini.

I took in her shoulder-length wavy brown hair, cute nerdy glasses, and body-hugging V-neck red dress. She looked to be in her mid-40s and was quite fit. I thought she might be of Italian heritage. She had mid-size breasts, and I could actually see her hard nipples poking through the fabric.

"I mean, does anyone actually do that?" I asked, and noticed some activity in my pants as my dick responded to her call to action. "How do they get away with it?"

She leaned toward me to whisper in my ear, and I confirmed that she was braless by placing my hand gently on her back. My body tingled with arousal. "Let me show you," she whispered.

I was several glasses of beer in at this point, and my brain offered no logical reason to say no to her. My member was pulsing with anticipation. I grabbed the dark blue airplane blanket to cover my erect penis, and the woman reached her hand into my lap and started to stroke my cock through my trousers.

"Uhh…" I moaned, without consciously realizing it.

She giggled and said, "Shh." The two of us were the only ones in our row of business class, and the man in the row in front of us had fallen asleep against the window and was snoring. The plane lights were dimmed, and the flight attendants were strapped into their seats at the front and back of the plane. The flight was scheduled to land in Denver around 9 PM, and it was already dark outside.

The sexy woman grabbed my chin and kissed me on the lips. I sloppily moved my tongue in and out of her mouth, and she nibbled my lip while she continued to rub my now fully erect dick.

"Come with me," she said, and grabbed my hand. "And don't say a word." She stuck her head into the aisle and looked both ways, waiting until everyone was seated. Then she stood up, and I noticed her full ass bouncing as she walked down the aisle in provocative red heels.

Suddenly the plane hit a bit of turbulence. I stumbled a bit and almost fell into an empty seat, but the mystery woman pulled me forward and then stealthily opened and entered the bathroom without the flight attendants noticing.

The two of us were tightly crammed into the lavatory, but this lady knew what she was doing. She guided me to rotate my body so that I sat on the toilet.

"Pull out your cock," she said. "And spit on it for lubricant. Get ready to join the mile-high club, baby!"

I did as I was told and watched the enigmatic woman bend forward and lift up the skirt of her short red dress. She had a lacy black thong underneath. She could barely fit into the space in front of me, and there wasn't much room to move, so she straddled me and pressed her arms against the opposite wall. She pulled her thong aside and grabbed my hard penis, then guided her wet pussy down onto my member.

"Uhhhh…" I groaned again.

"Mmmm, yeah…" she said, and started riding my cock, lifting her pussy up and pressing it down, pumping herself on my dick. I reached my hands around and played with her boobs, pinching her nipples between my fingers and twisting. She moaned and pressed herself down on my member with more vigor, pumping up and down and up and down. Before long, I felt the inner walls of her pussy pulsing, and my dick felt completely engorged with my lust for her. She rode my hardness easily now, as our wet juices intermingled and even soaked my pants.

I was beyond caring about social graces. "Ride me," I told her.

"Yes, sir," she giggled, and pumped her pussy on my erect penis. Then suddenly she stopped, and her eyes rolled back in her head. Her body relaxed in my arms, and I felt my cock pulse and shoot my seed inside of her. Suddenly, the plane tilted, and the alcohol began to rise up in my body. I lost all sense of balance and unexpectedly threw up—all over my lap.

"Ew!" my new friend squealed. "I'm getting out of here!" She pulled her skirt down and fled. I locked the door behind her.

Shit, I thought. *What the hell can I wear now?* The plane tilted the other direction, causing me to heave again. The tiny plane lavatory was a mess, and so was I. I wasn't sure whether to drunkenly laugh or cry.

"Oh!" I shouted as I turned and went face first over the toilet. I ejected a stream of beer-scented vomit—were those the free airplane peanuts?—into the silver metal airplane toilet. The plane hit some more turbulence, and I hurled one more time. After the purging, I felt better, although my pants were soiled, and my logical mind was beginning to kick in and criticize my choices.

Did I really just sleep with another woman without a condom? I'd taken enough biology in high school to know that unprotected sex carried a few different risks, from unplanned pregnancy to STDs. But I had enough to worry about right now, so I pushed these thoughts out of my mind.

I had no other clothing with me, so I re-zipped my pants and tried to use the bathroom soap and brown paper towels to clean out the vomit spots. It looked like I had wet myself, but at least the stench had vanished. I used some water to wash out my mouth, and then drank a few handfuls to try to sober up. When I left the bathroom, I grabbed a copy of *Conde Nast* and used it to cover the wet spots on my crotch.

The woman in the red dress had grabbed her stuff and moved to the empty seat across the aisle. She looked like she had fallen asleep. I covered myself with the blanket and did the same, still feeling a bit queasy.

I'm such an idiot, I thought. *What Mistress would want me now?* With sadness heavy on my heart, I tried to sleep for the remainder of the flight. I felt a warm tear creep down the side of my nose when I closed my eyes. This was so embarrassing. *Maybe when I wake up, I'll discover it was all just a dream...* I thought.

"I may seem like a dream, but I'm your worst nightmare," said a woman's voice in my thoughts. The eyes from the *Kinky Times* advertisement flashed through my mind. *"And trust me, I know what you just did. I know who you are, who you want to be, and who you could be. But do you know yourself?"*

What the—oh well... My thoughts trailed off as I drifted into a shallow sleep. The plane soared forward toward Denver.

I jolted awake when the plane's wheels hit the runway at Denver International Airport. My nostrils filled with the aroma of vomit, and my head felt like it was stuffed with cotton. I couldn't remember what had happened before I passed out, but when I looked down at my lap, I saw a crusty stain coating my crotch.

Holy hell! I thought. *What have I done?* An icky sense of guilt felt heavy around my gut. My eyes darted around the plane, and I noticed the hot brown-haired woman seated across the row from me avoided making eye contact. I plastered a smile on my face and tried to appear unperturbed.

I didn't have any extra clothing packed in my carry-on bag, so I planned to cover my dirty trousers with my briefcase until I could get my checked bag. There was no way I could let the Mistresses see me in this state! I wanted to make an excellent first impression because I'd been waiting for this opportunity my entire life.

Even as a young man, I had fantasized about having a strong woman telling me what to do. When I turned 18 and got an internship at an office job, I got off every night imagining my sexy female boss instructing me on how to pleasure her with my tongue and hands. I noticed it was the feeling of submission that pleased me the most, even more than the impression of her sexy form, taste, or voice. I loved surrendering my will to hers. It gave me relief from the pressure of "being a man."

I had to grow up faster than most because my mother abandoned me as a baby. A very wealthy and well-connected family on the Upper East Side of New York City had adopted me, and the same nanny that raised their three kids raised me. While they were kind, the couple was rarely home. They were both hard-working account managers in financial services in the city, and they'd grown wealthy through diligent effort.

Thinking about my childhood, I suddenly wanted a beer. *Maybe I can stop at the airport bar,* I mused. *No way, man!* shouted a voice from my Higher Self. *You've already had plenty to drink. Clean yourself up for the Mistresses and hit the road!*

I felt like I was caught between an angel and a devil sitting on my shoulders again. Part of me craved some comfort from a nice cold Guinness. The other part was still concerned about my filthy pants and the fact I'd blacked out the night before.

For once, I went with the angel. Instead of going to the bar, I awkwardly waited for my checked bag by the baggage carousel, while clasping my rectangular leather briefcase strategically over my lower half. I stayed as far from others as I could, in case they could smell me. I saw a few folks dart their eyes toward me and wondered if they knew what had happened.

When I spotted my bag coming down the conveyer belt, I quickly grabbed it and accidentally bumped the woman with the brown hair.

"My apologies, miss," I said.

"Don't bother," she said sharply, and backed away. She was looking at me like I was infectious or dangerous. I couldn't understand why. *Oh well. Not everyone's going to love you,* I thought to myself. I briskly walked to the bathroom and wheeled my luggage into the steel metal stall.

I had a pair of pressed brown trousers on the top of my suitcase. I sat on the toilet so I could remove the nasty pants. Then I pulled on the pressed trousers and inspected my appearance in the full-length mirror. I figured I looked presentable. I knew it was wasteful, but I was so ashamed of the vomit pants, I just threw them away, washed my hands, checked my appearance in the mirror, and left the bathroom. I shook my head. Those designer pants had cost me $500. Oh well... I walked outside into the cool Denver night, where a car would be waiting to pick me up along with some of the other New Recruits.

I got into the back of a sleek limo that was filled with nine other men. The first man must've been exceptionally tall. I noticed he had awkwardly pulled his giant legs into the backseat of the limo. The extremely long-legged African-American man, who had sculpted arm muscles and solid abs, stuck out his hand for me to shake. His short black hair had a hint of gray, and his smile lit up his kind face. I noticed some wrinkles around his eyes and mouth.

"The name's Fred," he said, and I thought I heard a slight Southern drawl. "Nice to meet you."

"Theodore," I said.

Next to Fred sat a man of Asian descent who looked quite strong. His professional clothing and grooming were immaculate. He had short black hair and was quite clean-cut.

"Andrew," he said, and offered a fist bump.

"Nice to meet you," I replied and returned the fist

bump.

"Brandon," said the tan man seated next to Andrew. I was already losing track of their names. I had a bit of a brain fog after the flight. Plus, checking out Brandon's muscles made me feel a bit insecure. *Why would the Mistresses choose me over him?* I thought, and had a brief flash of embarrassment remembering the vomit pants and my blackout on the plane.

"Nice to meet you, too," I said. The limo featured plush velvet seats, and the men were squeezed in pretty tight so that they could all fit.

"Aloha, man! I'm Kahua," said a booming and bold voice that emanated from a man with a big broad chest and big round belly. "From Hawaii. It's going to be tough adjusting to the cold!"

"For sure, dude. Good luck," I said. "I'm from New England, so the cold climate is normal for me." *Maybe that will give me an advantage?* I feebly hoped.

"I'm from England proper, mate," said a pale, lanky man with a mop of curly black hair. He had a definite British accent. "The name's Oliver."

"Hi, Oliver," I said. *That dude barely looks 18! I* thought. *And my pudgy stomach looks even worse next to his scrawny ass. Plus, ladies love British accents! How am I going to pull this one off?*

"Hey buddy, my name is Leonard. Leonard Lopez, Jr. I'm from L.A," said a tanned older man with dark hair slicked down. He had a few gray hairs and wrinkles around his eyes and mouth. Gold earrings studded with diamonds glinted on his ears.

"Nice jewelry, man," I said.

"Love the Rolex, bro," Leonard replied.

"Thanks!" I said. For a moment, I felt a sense of relief that the men seemed pretty open and friendly.

"The name's Thomas," said a young white man with red hair and freckles. He stuck out his hand, and I shook it.

"William," said a stocky and short balding man with Indian features and a strong British accent. "You look like a nutter. Your shirt doesn't match your pants or shoes or belt." William pointedly eyed my ensemble, looking me up and down. His sharp green eyes contrasted with his dark tan skin and thick black eyebrows and mustache.

I glanced down and realized William was right. I hadn't thought about mixing brown and black when I'd grabbed the top pair of pants from my suitcase, but now it was obvious the two shades were not meant to mix with this outfit. My insecurity grew, and I started nervously scratching my leg.

"What are you? The fashion police?" I snapped. The only ones I wanted policing me in Denver were the dominatrixes! I hoped they had handcuffs…

Another balding man, this one almost completely nondescript, held out a pudgy hand for a handshake. He looked like a dude you'd stumble across in an elevator in a stuffy office building.

"Last, but not least, I'm Carl," he stated.

"Good to meet you," I said, and squeezed into the last seat. "Are there beers in that mini fridge?"

"Let's find out," Fred said. He opened the fridge and pulled out a 12-pack. "Hey, it's fully stocked with a local Denver microbrew for each of us."

Fred handed a beer to each of the men, popped his drink open, and held it up. "Cheers, fellows!"

All ten of us clinked cans, then chugged. I imagined I wasn't the only one who was nervous. I drank quickly because part of me wanted to throw up again just from smelling the beer.

By the time we arrived at Mile High Stadium, it was getting late. Our car pulled up behind a long line of limos. I counted them. 1, 2, 3, 4, 5, 6, 7, 8, 9, 10, 11! Eleven limos... *Were they all filled with 10 men?* I wondered. I watched the other limos disembark and counted. The limo in front of me only had five men; otherwise, they all had 10. So, I was suddenly one New Recruit among 105 men, each with their own strengths and weaknesses. *How on earth was I going to stand out?* I wondered how many had applied and why my application had made it through.

I wished my spot as a submissive in the Mistresses'

stable was guaranteed, but I knew better than to count on it. I decided to devote myself wholeheartedly to selfless service and complete submission. I vowed to do the best I could to outperform the other men and impress the powerful (and hot) Mistresses.

When it was my turn to get out of the car, a well-groomed sissy maid guided me to a long folding table. The beautiful being looked extremely feminine, but had masculine broad shoulders and towered over me. The sissy maid had full make-up and wore their hair in pigtails. Their body was laced into a tight white vinyl corset over a mound of fluffy short sheer light pink petticoats with ruffles. I got a glimpse of something metallic and silver underneath the petticoats and wondered what it could be. They also wore elegant soft white leather mid-length gloves.

"Last name?" asked the sissy maid.

"Thompson," I said.

"T, right there," the sissy maid directed me to another fabulous sissy maid who was sitting behind a sign that said "R–Z."

This feminized maid also had full makeup, including ruby red lips. She wore a tight red sequined dress and red sequin stiletto boots. She wore a red feather boa and a red curly wig. She extended a hand gloved in red satin and said, "Pleasure to meet you. You can call me sissy Rita." I thought she looked quite glamorous and wondered if I might get to play around with makeup someday.

"Sign this waiver, and give us your driver's license so we can make a copy," the sissy in sequins stated.

"Here you go," I said.

"You'll get used to saying 'Yes, Mistress,' soon," the sissy maid said before leaving to copy the license.

I read the waiver and in particular noticed the following alert:

> "You, the undersigned, hereby surrender any and all legal recourse against Mistress Insomnia, Mistress Intrigue, and Mistress Doom. You hereby accept full and complete responsibility for any and all consequences that come from your submission and presence at Femdom Boot Camp. All Femdom Boot Camp activities will be sane, safe, and consensual. You are welcome to leave or terminate any scene at any time. You will be trained on proper use of safe words and are expected to use them when necessary."

The waiver ended by listing potential risks and one potential reward:

- Emotional Distress
- Physical Pain
- Humiliation
- Chastity and Orgasm Restriction
- Financial Ruin
- Loss of Ego-Self and Identity
- Opening to Your Truest Self

"Signing this waiver indicates your acceptance of these risks, along with any that have not been explicitly mentioned. You, the undersigned, enter Femdom Boot Camp at your own risk. You are welcome to leave at any time, and may be removed from the experience at any time without a refund for your money or time."

I gulped, grabbed a pen, and signed. I hoped for the best, but feared for the worst. I handed the contract to the red-haired maid, and noticed my hand was shaking.

"Now get your booty inside to get fitted for your outfit!" the maid squealed and eyed me up and down. "I think it'll look pretty good on you, but you might want to cut back on the booze to really impress the Mistresses."

My hand went down to my protruding belly. I almost looked pregnant. I was embarrassed but had to admit this person had a good point, especially after my drinking binge last night. A little beer burp erupted from my lips before I could reply. I covered my mouth and stepped inside the locker room, ready for my uniform fitting.

The glamorous sissy maid wearing the white vinyl corset was managing the cock cage fitting in the locker room. "You've all signed your waivers," she announced. "You can call me sissy Charlene. I am the sissy maid manager in charge of your intake process. Now it's time to get ready for the loincloth lineup."

Yet again I wondered, *why on earth did I answer that ad?* I looked around nervously. The 100+ other men were all listening to sissy Charlene's instructions with rapt attention.

She continued: "You've each been given a locker number and a key hanging on a dog tag. You are responsible for wearing this key for the duration of your stay with us here at Femdom Boot Camp. You are New Recruits and this is basic training. And, trust me, you'd better get a solid grasp of the basics of submission quick, or you'll get booted from Femdom Boot Camp. Those Mistresses don't play games. You're not in the patriarchy any more, boys."

Some other sissies had come into the locker room and were standing behind sissy Charlene. I recognized sissy Rita in red sequins and saw an unfamiliar sissy who was dressed like a sexy schoolgirl. sissy Rita laughed knowingly at sissy Charlene's comment.

sissy Charlene continued her instructions: "Go to your locker and strip naked, then shower off and shave your balls completely. After you dry off and put your belongings in your locker, line up to prepare for the loincloth and chastity cage fitting."

I gulped. Soon I would no longer be a free man. *Would I be able to handle not being in charge for once?*

sissy Charlene added, "We will start slow at first and let you remove the cages at night while you get adjusted to this lifestyle. The sissies will hold onto the keys, and we take this duty very seriously. Gentlemen, get naked and get in line."

The sissy wearing a short plaid skirt gave me my dog tag, which was printed with the number 47N. This would match both my locker number and my yard line location out on the field.

I found the matching locker and started stripping down. I felt a bit embarrassed to get naked in front of total strangers that I was competing against, but I acted like I was just at the gym, took care of my business, and tried not to stare at anyone else.

I couldn't help but notice that scrawny dude's package, though. The tall guy, Oliver, had already stripped bare, and I caught sight of his well-shaped penis dangling above some quite juicy balls when the young man walked by my locker on the way to the fitting line.

At least the color of my belt, shoes, and pants won't matter anymore, I thought. My ego was still a bit stung by what that jerk had said in the limo. I had to admit all of my insecurities were coming up in this moment, and I felt a bit like puking. I was nervous about my physical body and how the other men and Mistresses would see it. I also worried a bit about the training. Would I physically be able to handle it? I knew real-life Army Boot Camp was tough but had no clue what Femdom Boot Camp would be like.

I hope it includes plenty of knee-high leather boots, handcuffs, whippings, and spankings, I thought, and without consciously realizing it, started stroking my cock.

"Whoa, Bro. I need to get by to my locker," said the booming voice of the Hawaiian man, Kahua, from behind me. I startled. I wasn't sure if Kahua had seen me jerking off.

"Oh, yeah. Sure. Of course," I replied, and started nervously scratching my arm. *At least there's one dude here who looks more pregnant than I do…* I thought.

Superficial. So superficial. A female voice suddenly echoed in my mind. Instead of hearing my own voice narrating my inner dialogue, the sharp and bold woman's voice arose within my own thoughts in my head; my mind raced as a vision of the Mistress's eyes from the *Kinky Times* ad filled my mind's eye.

Huh? What th—? I was getting flustered now. Was this woman reading my thoughts or what? I'd never even met her, but I kept feeling like…she was watching me somehow, from inside my own mind.

My cock was completely flaccid now, and I felt similarly deflated. I shoved my luggage in the locker and put my key on my wrist.

An extremely attractive and exceptionally tall man with dark curly hair and olive skin was getting undressed at the locker next to me. I had to tilt my head up to even see his face! At 5′9″ I'm not typically the tallest guy in a group, but I don't usually feel as short as I did next to this dude. I grew even more insecure as I ogled the man's perfectly chiseled chest, stunning muscular arms, and tight ass. He was like a model of the ideal male specimen. The guy had giant thighs and six-pack abs. On the other hand, my gut looked like I drank a six-pack daily.

"You look like a personal trainer," I said. *Or a demi-god,* I thought.

"Ha! I am one," the man replied. "The name's Billy. Billy Button."

"Oh, cool. My name's Theodore Thompson. Where are you from?" I was suddenly acutely aware that I was naked, and I couldn't help wondering what Billy thought about my appearance.

"I live in San Francisco," Billy said.

"Nice to meet you," I stated.

The sissy maid at the entrance had given each New

Recruit a backpack filled with essentials. It included a one-size-fits-all pair of hot pink flip-flops for the shower as well as a luxurious lavender- and rose-scented body wash.

Heck, maybe submitting to powerful women wouldn't be so bad after all! I welcomed the opportunity to clean myself off after my rough flight, and I appreciated the feminine touches. I always bought men's body wash, even though I hated the smell. I was too embarrassed to purchase the much more appealing floral and vanilla scents in the women's aisle.

I grabbed the loofah on a rope, body wash, and a razor with shaving cream. Then I put on the hot pink flip-flops and shuffled to the shower. It was a large, room with multiple shower heads. I could see 10 or 15 men lathering up and cleaning their bodies from head to toe, each one wearing only hot pink sandals.

I wasn't sure whether to look or not look at the other men's members, so I awkwardly checked out their packages with short bursts of my eyes left and right while I lathered up. Everyone was scrubbing hard and taking care to completely shave their balls and nether regions. They clearly wanted to impress the Mistresses.

A short, pudgy man was lifting his penis and scrutinizing his ball sack to make sure he had fully removed every last hair. The Hawaiian man was shaving his chest and had already taken care of the hair down there. Kahua turned to ask Oliver, the pale scrawny man behind me, to shave his back.

"Is that required?" I asked. I actually liked my body hair and didn't really want to remove any of it. I had a bit of a 5-o-clock shadow happening now that I'd been out of the office for a few days, and I thought it made me look so sexy, rugged, and masculine. I hoped the Mistresses wouldn't make me be completely clean-shaven.

"They only told us that we had to shave our nether regions for the Boot Camp, but I believe the ladies will love it if I give myself the full body shave treatment," Kahua said. "I'm going to make my first impression smooth and clean."

"Mm-hmm," I mumbled, then turned slightly away from the other men. I lathered up and enjoyed the beautiful aroma of lavender and rose filling the steamy shower. Every once in a while, I caught a glimpse of a nice, tight ass or a particularly appealing dick, and I noticed I got a bit turned on.

I've never been with a man before, but I am not opposed to it. Primarily social pressures led to me dating women. It definitely seems easier to conform to heteronormativity, especially since my adopted parents are staunch Catholics who taught that sex between two men is sinful. I never really believed it, and I managed to throw off most of the external religious practices once I found Zen in college. Zen Buddhism sounded respectable enough that my adoptive parents accepted it as a valid religion on par with Catholicism.

But exploring sexual relationships with men makes me nervous. I worry if I am strong enough to be openly bisexual. Part of me wants to be totally uninhibited, and the other part feels I must stay "socially acceptable" for my everyday life. I yearn to be let completely free here with the Mistresses, to be fully sexually uninhibited. I hope to be able to serve all three. I also wonder if I might be asked to be with another man during my time here. I think I would enjoy that, but it is definitely outside my comfort zone and experience.

So, despite having a hangover and jet lag, I somehow managed to shave my pubic hair without drawing blood. I felt extremely vulnerable shaving myself in front of the other men, and I went as quickly as I could without hurting myself. I'd never noticed the odd blue veins or the slightly darker purple tint of my ball sack until now. I felt extremely self-conscious, though I noted everyone's cock and physique looked totally different and unique. Very few New Recruits had the ideal of male perfection, though a couple were definitely athletes and physical trainers. Most looked like the typical sedentary American man who drives to work and sits at a desk all day.

Once I'd shaved myself clean, I used the loofah to spread the luxurious soap all over my body. I scrubbed my slightly hairy chest and my big belly, including the pleasure trail down to my cock.... It felt good to touch myself down there again. It had been a while since I'd masturbated. And through the steam, I could see men of all ages, shapes, and sizes with naked butts and dicks hanging out all around me. It seemed there were dozens of men who slipped into the shower, soaped up, shaved, and went on to the next phase while I took my time savoring the sensual experience, fragrance, and sexy view through the mist in the shower.

I wanted to smell amazing from head to toe to impress the Mistresses, so I got every crack and crevice on my body lathered up. As I did a second round over my protruding gut, my sideward glance caught Billy's six-pack and flat, strong chest covered in soap. For a moment, I fantasized about helping Billy rub the soap all over his body and wondered what it would feel like to touch Billy's muscular bubble butt.

Billy noticed me staring and cleared his throat.

"Huh?" I came back to reality only to notice my hand had been unconsciously creeping toward my penis as I fantasized about Billy. I suddenly wondered if I was even allowed to masturbate at all here. Wasn't that some femdom thing? I had watched a few pornos, read some magazines, but never actually met a person in real life who was into this, so I wasn't totally sure what to expect.

At home, masturbation added spice to my rather dull life and helped me escape the pain I'd inherited due to the circumstances surrounding my upbringing, namely my birth mother's abandonment. I did not know why she put me up for adoption at Catholic Adoption Services, only that she was rather young and lived in Queens when she did. I imagined she felt incapable of caring for me for some reason, or possibly even shamed or traumatized by the manner of her pregnancy. Logically, I felt for her, and had compassion for whatever she'd been through. Emotionally, my inner child wondered why mommy rejected me, and I grieved, for I did not even know if she was alive or dead today. I felt I could never know who I truly was since I did not know who brought me into this world. I'd definitely never met my father either. For all I knew, he was the scum of the earth.

This hollow pit followed me everywhere I went, and I tried to fill it with money, sex, and drugs, like a living Wall Street stereotype. But as profitable as my trade was, I did not feel particularly fulfilled by my daily grind. And my love life was pitiful. After my college girlfriend had unceremoniously dumped me by ghosting me after graduation, my heart and trust in women had been broken. My abandonment wound was triggered so deeply, I ended up sobbing and pounding my fists on the floor, angry that she had left me forever. I felt like a discarded baby, crying and alone, my nose filled with snot, and my room filled with crumpled tissues soaked from wiping my tears. Love felt so painful that I didn't seek any true intimacy and tried to entertain myself with beer, jerking off to porn, and random sexual encounters instead.

Feeling awkward around Billy now that I'd been caught jerking off, I shut off the water and went back to my locker with my loofah and soap. On my way to the locker, I heard a familiar voice say, "Hey, Theodore!" I swiveled my head and saw my former New York University fraternity brother Quinn Baker standing completely nude and waiting in line for the inspection and chastity cage fitting.

I blushed. I never expected to encounter anyone I knew here, much less someone I knew so well. We had even double-dated back in college! "I–I–I– had no idea you were into this," I stammered.

"Oh yeah, man. Didn't get into it until after I graduated from NYU. Didn't know you were into BDSM either," Quinn said. He had a bold, slightly husky voice and a very strong jaw line. He looked like a Greek Adonis, with dark blonde curls that framed his face. I gasped when he looked at me with his piercing green eyes. Standing at 5'12", Quinn was slightly taller, but close to my height at 5'9". He had been an athlete in college, and Quinn still looked like he worked out a lot more frequently than I did. My mouth watered a bit looking at him.

I cleared my throat and said, "I always had a overwhelming desire to submit to a strong and powerful woman, but I tried so hard to fit in and be normal, I tried to suppress my desire."

"I know what that's like," Quinn sighed and glanced at my wet, nude body. I still hadn't had a chance to dry off.

Is he checking me out? The rules of the world as I knew them were quickly vanishing here in Femdom Boot Camp. I continued, "I was too nervous to pursue it before now, but when I saw the *Kinky Times* ad, I felt called to follow it, to be brave and to do what I believed in, without care for what others would think."

"Something about that ad really called out to me, too," Quinn smiled, and I grinned back.

"I wonder what we've signed up for…" I said. My voice rose to a higher pitch and squeaked at the end of my sentence, and I blushed. Seeing Quinn here, naked and looking like a Greek statue, I felt like a teenage boy with a majorly taboo crush. I giggled nervously, and my cock and belly jiggled a bit. I blushed and hurried back to my locker to towel off.

I felt the slightly cool air in the locker room touch my damp skin, and my penis bounced up and down as I moved. I imagined Quinn staring at my flat, white ass as I retreated. I focused on my breath and tried to calm my excitement as I used the key hanging from my neck to undo the locker.

I hung up the loofah and placed the soap in a shower caddy inside the locker, then began drying myself off with the towel that had been placed inside. First, I pulled up my legs and dried my calves and thighs. As I bent over to get under my thighs, I heard Quinn's throaty voice behind me. "Want some help?" he asked.

"Uh, s-s-sure!" I said. Quinn winked at me and grabbed my towel, then used it to dry my back. "Thank you so much," I added. He moved lower with the towel, and vigorously patted my ass and cock dry. He giggled as my dick started to rise a bit with arousal.

"Excuse me!" a stern voice called from the other end of the locker room. I noticed every man's head swiveled to listen, and saw many had already been watching Quinn and I. An attractive, tall sissy maid that I hadn't seen yet pursed her hot pink lips and batted her (probably false) eyelashes at us. "This is inspection and cock cage fitting time, NOT time for your erotic experience. Hurry up and get in line!"

I felt a bit uncomfortable in my new environment. As open-minded as I thought I was, I did not quite know what to think about the male dressed as a feminized sissy maid who had just spoken.

At first, I'd even thought there was a woman in the locker room, because this man wore an over-the-top frilly maid uniform with multiple petticoats and a boned corset. He had long brown hair and was shaved from head to toe (as far as I could tell). The maid skirt had black sheer fabric, so I could see that the sissy wore a hot pink lace thong under the skirt. The maid had on black silk thigh-high stockings with lace borders. His makeup was impeccable. *That might be me one day,* I thought, and blushed. This was so different from the frat world at NYU or the boy's club on Wall Street already.

I trudged to my spot in line to start the process with sissy Rita, who stood tall in her glittery red platform boots. The other New Recruits were in various phases of being fitted for their chastity cages and suede loincloths. Quinn and I were some of the last remaining who had not been fitted.

sissy Rita had pulled in her rather stocky and masculine bulk with a boned corset over the brilliant red sequin dress. Her monochromatic look was somewhere between '80s prom glamour and Vegas showgirl dazzle, and her demeanor was exacting and disciplined.

I felt extremely nervous, and walked with mindful, slow steps, my eyes downcast. Would I be found suitable to start Boot Camp with the Mistresses? I was so intrigued and filled with desire. I hoped I had not wasted my time or money coming here...

sissy Rita checked my name and my locker number on my dog tag. "Continue to wear this around your neck so that you know where you belong," sissy Rita told me. "From here on out, you will be known as boy, slave, or simply your yard line number. Are you ready to leave Theodore Thompson behind?"

"Yes, ma'am," I said confidently, though inside, I was not so sure. I glanced at the number 47N printed on the dog tag, which hung on a sterling silver bead ball chain around my neck. It looked just like an Army dog tag, except the back read "Property of

Femdom Boot Camp Arousal Army."

Another sissy maid stood towering at the next stop in the line. sissy Phyllis was about 5'11" normally, but her 6-inch heels made her 6'5" tall. Her coppery red hair seemed to be a wig, and she was wearing a cute dark blue and green plaid pleated skirt with a starched white button-up shirt on top. I could see the bright red lace of her bulging bra through the somewhat sheer fabric of the blouse, and she appeared to have a quite full bosom.

The beautiful sissy maid was measuring each man's penis length and girth with a measuring tape. sissy maid Phyllis took down notes with the measurements, then grabbed the appropriately sized stainless-steel cock ring from three options and guided each man how to put it on.

Quinn and I watched about 10 men point their penis down and slip it through the ring, then pass their testicles through, one ball at a time. Some men had to push and squeeze their flaccid cocks to get them fitted in a tighter ring. I couldn't help but wonder if the Mistresses would prefer the men with girthy penises. If so, I was at an advantage! My past girlfriends loved my thickness. One even told me she was addicted to my dick. I got the largest ring, which was around two inches in diameter.

sissy Phyllis motioned to me to step forward for my fitting, and sissy Charlene took over. While sissy

Charlene was wrapping a measuring tape around my solid six-incher, the sissy maid joked she was running out of measuring tape because my dick was so thick. I looked down and saw sissy Charlene's dark brown eyes outlined in thick kohl eyeliner looking into my own. I noticed my cock was growing hard with sissy Charlene's touch.

"Well, well, well, what have we here?" sissy Charlene asked. I heard Kahua holler. He had gone right in front of me in line, and he was about to get fitted for his loincloth with sissy Rita. I blushed. It seemed I was already beginning to make an impression on the group.

"Uh, um…" I started wringing my hands and tried to figure out what to say.

"Doesn't matter," sissy Charlene said. "But I can't fit you until you soften up. Go think about something that'll calm you down and come back to get fitted later.

"Yes, sissy Charlene," I said obediently.

Kahua moved forward to receive his suede loincloth while I retreated to a locker room bench to cool off.

"I'm sissy Rita, and I'll be taking your loincloth measurements," said the fabulously adorned sissy maid in the red sequin dress.

"Thank you, sissy Rita," said Kahua.

Rita wrapped the suede buckskin loincloth around

Kahua wide waist. The tan loincloth had a thick strap that hung down in front of Kahua's package and another one that covered his butt crack. I looked up from my spot on the bench and noticed Kahua's strong thighs bulging out from the sides of the loincloth. As he walked, I caught a glimpse of the cock cage Kahua now wore fitted around his balls and penis. He was walking kind of funny and seemed a bit stiff.

"How's it feel?" I asked.

"Honestly, pretty cold," Kahua said, and laughed. "But we'll get used to it."

"Theodore, has your erection died down yet?" sissy Charlene hollered from across the locker room.

"Yes, sissy Charlene," I replied.

"Then get that booty back over here," sissy Charlene said. "It's time for your fitting. Try to think of something non-erotic like baseball or a freezing cold shower, OK, buddy?"

"Ha, ha, yeah, sure," I said, and felt mildly embarrassed. But I tried to focus my thoughts on something completely unerotic, the harsh Mother Nun from my boyhood Catholic school. She always wore frumpy, ill-fitted gowns, and she was quick to verbally humiliate any boy she felt was not up to snuff. I had hated her. I didn't really want to be thinking of her right now, but I was willing to do whatever it took to get an introduction to these Mistresses. And I had to be soft to be fitted, and I had to be fitted to go in, so…

"Brr," I said. sissy Charlene had placed the cock ring around my shaft, added the stainless-steel cage that wrapped cruelly around my girthy penis (my male pride and joy), then locked the contraption shut. I felt a bit confined and restricted when I heard the lock close. Suddenly I felt nervous and trapped. *Would I really be able to get out of this if I needed to? Was there I chance I might never touch my penis again after this moment?* I nervously scratched my thigh.

I asked, "Is it supposed to be this tight?"

"Try it for a while and see what you think," sissy Charlene said. "It does need to be snug, but we don't want it to be terribly uncomfortable because you're going to be wearing that for quite some time if you stick around here. If it's too tight we can refit you tomorrow. Now get your loincloth on and get out there, buddy!"

sissy Charlene directed us to the next station, where sissy Rita was measuring each man's hips and giving them a leather loincloth to wear. The glamourous sissy said, "Gentlemen, take your loincloths! Real suede for some real submissives. This, along with your cock cage and dog tag, will be your uniform for Femdom Boot Camp. That'll really toughen you up when it gets to be October!"

I glanced around at the group of New Recruits and caught Kahua's eye. Kahua was clad in a buckskin loincloth and had already been fitted with his cock cage. I could see the ring fit snugly against Kahua's balls, and the man's modest cock had been secured in the metal chastity device. *How will this stainless steel feel in the cold Colorado fall weather?* I wondered, and felt a sense of dread.

Kahua mimicked teeth chattering and wrapped his arms around himself as if trying to keep himself warm. "I just hope those Mistresses are hot enough to keep me warm this October," he said, and a few men laughed and hollered.

"Hey, New Recruit!" sissy Charlene screamed. "Don't let the Mistresses hear you objectifying and sexualizing them like that. They simply will not tolerate it. We submissives exist to serve them, and our only purpose in life is to bring them pleasure. Drop this patriarchal bullshit that sees women as objects for your use."

"Hey man, I was only kidding," Kahua said and eyed sissy Charlene's white vinyl corset and light pink lipstick with a bit of jealousy. Kahua had to admit sissy Charlene was both glamorous and terrifying in this moment. sissy Charlene looked extremely tall in her white patent leather platform Mary Janes. Kahua had not been disciplined like this since he was a child. As a grown man who hunted wild pigs and managed a group of luxury resorts in Hawaii, Kahua was used to being the man in charge.

"Call me sissy Charlene, NOT 'man.' I don't associate myself with that disgusting gender. Remember, you are here to serve these Mistresses, and you need to leave your ego at the door," sissy Charlene added with a bit of a sneer. "And trust me, I am their eyes and ears when the Mistresses are not around. Keep your words impeccable if you want to stay in the Mistress's good graces."

"Yes, sir," said Kahua.

"I said, call me sissy," said sissy Charlene. "Or sissy Charlene."

"Yes, sissy Charlene," said Kahua.

"Thank you. That's more like it, New Recruit!"

I stopped by sissy Rita, and she wrapped the buckskin suede loincloth around my hips. As she leaned in, I caught a whiff of her floral perfume. It smelled lovely, like jasmine. For a moment, I thought of the fragrant flowers outside my New Jersey suburban home. Right now, that life seemed so far away from me.

Here I was, at Femdom Boot Camp, face to face with a beautiful sissy, whom I assumed had been forced into feminization by these strong dominatrixes. My mind was already blown, and I had only just arrived. I couldn't wait to see the Mistresses themselves!

I hoped they were wearing leather, like I now was. It felt amazing against my skin. sissy Rita laced on the suede loincloth with leather ties so that it stayed snug around my body. I felt a bit awkward feeling the breeze on my sack and penis, but knowing others could peep a view actually turned me on. Now, when my penis pulsed with arousal, the cold steel cage quickly zapped my erotic impulse and sent me spiraling into a sensation of pain. I felt pretty uncomfortable in my metal chastity device. I wondered how I could handle wearing this; after all, I usually masturbated several times a day!

"Do you wear one of these?" I asked sissy Rita.

"Been caged for 24 years, and it's the best decision I ever made," the maid said.

"Why's that?" I asked. This guy looked young to have been caged for 24 years. Maybe it was his makeup?

"One word—liberation," sissy Rita said with certainty and winked at me.

"Huh," I mused. "Liberation through extreme restraint."

The sissy maid ran her hands down the boned corset and popped her hips and booty, making her sequined dress hug her curves. sissy Rita exclaimed, "Liberation through constraint? Mm-hmm, honey! One day you'll see for yourself."

I glanced at Quinn, and we made puzzled faces at each other. Even though I was trying to play it cool, I felt heat on my face. I was definitely blushing. Quinn and I giggled nervously.

Quinn was now getting fitted for his male chastity device. sissy Phyllis grabbed Quinn's limp dick and lubricated it with a bit of a rough touch. It looked like Quinn stifled a whimper as the glamorous sissy slid a cold metal cock ring over his limp penis and scrotum. The hard ring now touched Quinn's body.

I noticed that the sissy maid had on very severe makeup—dark maroon lipstick with full lip liner and a dark smoky eye—that seemed a bit too fancy for the Mile High Stadium locker room. In fact, I thought she looked more like a flight attendant than a glamorous sissy submissive.

But who was I to say anything? Our whole crew looked a bit out of place here. The walls featured photos of all-star Denver Broncos players from the past, and each locker was painted in the team colors. Some uniforms were on display. The football players in the photos looked super muscular because of the padding.

The group of New Recruits, on the other hand, was practically nude, with only a thin strip of leather covering our caged cocks. The sissy maids had some padding, too, but it was a bit different. One had a thick padded bra that added ample breasts to his frame, and the one fitting Quinn's cage was rocking some assertive 1980s shoulder pads under her button-up shirt.

sissy Charlene suddenly grabbed Quinn's limp dick and placed it in the cage. Quinn jumped a little as he felt the cold metal against his cock. At this point, he was naked except for the metal contraption between his legs. sissy Charlene lined up the locking pins and holes, and I saw Quinn gulp nervously as the lock clanked shut. There was a convenient urination hole so we wouldn't have to take them off to pee.

"Do we wear these the entire time?" Quinn asked nervously.

"I'd take it moment by moment, if I were you." sissy Charlene quipped. "Most of you won't last a week with these sadistic Mistresses."

Now that Quinn and I were both caged, we had a little room inside the device, but not enough space to become fully erect. I really wasn't sure how I was going to handle this. I was always horny and had plenty of erections normally throughout the day.

You'll need to master the discipline of mind and body to survive here, slave, Mistress Insomnia's voice entered my thoughts. I shivered and imagined the beautiful Mistress forcing me to bend over and spanking my bare behind with her leather riding crop. I felt my cock slowly expand until the chastity device stopped my full erection, and I felt an uncomfortable sensation in my loins. The feeling of cold metal on my sensitive skin also dampened my arousal. Before long, my hard-on had completely disappeared.

Next time catch yourself before it gets to that point, Mistress Insomnia advised in my thoughts.

"Yes, ma'am," I shouted, and saluted by placing my hand on my forehead.

"What the heck, man?" Quinn laughed. "You talking to yourself?"

The sissies stopped their chatter and turned to look at us. sissy Charlene put her hands on her hips and stared at me. She still held the key to my chastity cage dangling from her gloved finger. sissy Phyllis raised an eyebrow and simply said, "Tsk, tsk."

I suddenly realized I had reacted to the thoughts as if I were receiving directions from the Mistress herself. But clearly she was not in the room, and no one else had heard her command. At this point I just equated the thoughts to her, although I suppose I might also be going insane. I suddenly realized I had no idea if I was hallucinating or receiving a telepathic message.

I hoped I would get some one-on-one time with Mistress Insomnia to figure it out! I would have to be on my best behavior to catch her attention. Although I was normally quite confident, I had to admit, in this environment, I felt extremely nervous and unsure of myself.

Having my cock in this cold steel cage didn't help. It felt withered and useless, and so did I. Did I really base this much of my self-confidence on my penis? I took a moment to contemplate that. In a way, it was sad how much of my pride and sense of identity was connected to my genitalia and its functioning.

I'd studied enough Buddhism to know all is impermanent, and that attachment can cause suffering. I knew that if I continued to associate my worth with my cock, I was in for a difficult road. After all, my penis would inevitably change, my sex drive would change, my body would change... *So, what is the point exactly?* I thought. My thoughts spiraled into nihilism, and ideas from the philosophers I'd studied in college filled my mind. For a moment, I was lost in my inner world.

I jumped as Quinn tapped my shoulder. I noticed his buff chest and shoulders. The dude's arm muscles were bulging. Quinn was a busy high-powered lawyer, so I didn't know how he made time to work out... I felt guilty that I couldn't say the same for myself.

I still couldn't get over the fact I knew someone here. Was I tripping? I felt like everything I considered to be normal was suddenly completely different. At first, I had felt acutely embarrassed when I saw Quinn, my fraternity brother from college. I had no idea the dude was into BDSM—but then again, Quinn didn't know I was into it either. I had been dating the "good girl" when I knew Quinn in college, after all. I had been pretty good buddies with Quinn, and we'd spent a few late nights discussing philosophy and the meaning of life.

We both liked sports and were good-natured and chummy, but neither one of us had admitted our sexual fantasies or fetishes to the other despite having lived through a few wild fraternity parties together. Quinn and I had even gone on double dates together back in the day.

I had a momentary flash to a mental image of me, my ex, Quinn, and Quinn's now ex-wife chugging beers at Drink It Down, a dive bar that catered to NYU students and was known to be especially lax in checking IDs.

Through my memory, I recalled that Quinn and I had been wearing NYU T-shirts and khakis with belts. Both of us wanted to move up in the world and loved to look affluent and successful even in our off time, so we tended to dress somewhat formally. Our dates looked cute in denim shorts and matching college shirts. We had just left the basketball game, and were celebrating the team's win with some beers.

Things had gotten kind of wild, I remembered. My good-girl girlfriend decided to be a bit naughty that night, maybe because of the jubilance in the air after the win. She snuck under the table and went down on me, and no one in the crowded bar seemed to notice or care except Quinn. I remember Quinn winked at me because he knew what was going on under the table.

We were all pretty tipsy—I had a bit more beer than the rest—so they just laughed and laughed and felt free from worry. That is, until the hangover the next day, of course. I doubted that's what sissy Rita had meant by "liberation."

Returning to earth from my dream world, I looked up and couldn't help but stare at Quinn's 9-inch cock squeezed into the relatively small metal chastity cage. Catching my eye, Quinn winked at me. I was excited now.

Now that Quinn and I were fully caged, we were ready to get out on the field. Dozens of caged, loincloth-clad men filled the locker room. A warm and sassy voice over the loudspeaker chirped: "Welcome to the selection process for the Arousal Army. Now that you have been fitted for your male chastity devices and loincloths, please leave all your other belongings, including shoes, in your locker. Then report directly to the yard line on your hangtag. Some men might need to double up on yard lines. Find your spot, stand still, and remain quiet until further direction. And remember, submissives are to be seen and not heard."

"Yes, Mistress!" I heard the sissy maid who had fitted my cock cage shout. "You hear that, boys? That's how you respond to direction around here. Try it after the next round of announcements."

The voice repeated the announcement. This time, Quinn and I joined in with a solid, "Yes, Mistress!" A short and stocky man standing next to us grunted and muttered under his breath, "Like I'd let that sissy jackass tell me what to say and when. He's not my Mistress, that's for sure." The man smelled oddly like cigars considering he was practically nude. He had tiny black curly hairs sprinkled across his chest. I found his appearance, smell, and attitude quite distasteful. Quinn caught my eye and rolled his eyes at the dude. How far did he really think he would get with an attitude like that around here?

"At least that's one less competitor for our spot, huh?" Quinn whispered to me.

I held up a finger to my lips to gesture for silence. After the attention I'd gotten in the locker room earlier, I didn't want to upset the Mistresses or the sissies. I had wanted a chance to embrace true submission for decades, so I was not going to give it up over idle gossip and speculation. In my mind's eye, I could already see myself, wearing a frilly light blue sissy maid uniform and fitting cock cages for the next round of New Recruits at next year's event at Mile High Stadium. The Mistresses had been running Femdom Boot Camp annually for 10 years, and I hoped to be their submissive slave for the next 10 years.

As I leave the locker room, I notice that my loincloth is a bit snug and the strip of suede between my legs barely hides my member. My ass crack is covered—barely—so long as I stay still. When I walk, the motion of my legs moves the flaps of the loincloth and reveals basically everything. I notice I have started biting my fingernails again, and try to stop; I feel a bit of anxiety in the pit of my stomach, which is churning.

I connect to my breath and slowly take a deep, measured breath to calm my nerves. I finger my Femdom Boot Camp dog tag and glance at the number: 47N. Walking side-by-side with Quinn, I exit the locker room and head to yard line 47 on the north side of the stadium facing the stage. I'm delighted to see that Quinn stands on yard line 46, right next to me!

It's vaguely disconcerting how it seems impossible to tell anyone's rank or position when they're half-naked and wearing loincloths. I've grown accustomed to assessing wealth and status by checking out cars, suits, and watches, but here, I don't see any of that.

There are over 100 dudes, butt naked except for two tiny flaps of rawhide barely covering their nether regions. Each man is standing on the yard lines of the stadium designated by their dog tags. Out of nowhere, I remember that we are all wearing chastity cages, and I can't help but giggle to myself. I never thought I'd live to see so many strong, successful, and powerful men stripped bare of their clothing, much less their access to their manhood!

My friends from the women's studies classes I took in college would eat this up! After growing up in

New York City with my rich adoptive parents, I had entered NYU as a finance major. I studied philosophy on the side, and I ended up completing a few women's studies survey classes as electives. I found myself drawn in by a dawning awareness of the patriarchy.

I learned women were once treated as property legally under the marriage contract, and that they had no economic rights, in addition to a lack of political rights or education. I learned that as late as the 1970s a woman could not get her own credit card without her husband's signature in the United States. At other points in history, women were denied the right to own property in their own name, pass on an inheritance, or have rights to their body or sexual choice within marriage.

But today, I stood amongst some of the wealthiest and most successful men in the world, and we were here at Mile High Stadium in Denver, Colorado, to compete against each other for the rare opportunity to be a bootlicker bitch to three powerful Mistresses.

Was this progress? What would my previous girlfriend think of me if she knew I was here? What about my mother? I felt a wave of sadness as I longed to know who she was and why she had given me up for adoption. I sighed. Some mysteries might never be solved.

Standing on yard line 47 North, I try to straighten

my posture, and I puff up my chest. To my right is Oliver, the scrawny, tall British man with a mop of dark curly hair I'd met in the limo. I swear I can see the guy's bony hips poking out of his loin cloth. The dude looks like he has to be 18. His British accent is thick, so he is difficult to understand.

Of course, my New Jersey-New York accent is equally baffling to Oliver, the British lad. My head is still spinning. *What is he doing here? He looks way too young and pitiful to satisfy the Mistresses.*

I found out later that Oliver had just started college in London, and then took a break in classes so he could answer the ad he saw in *Kinky Folks* magazine, which is distributed globally. Oliver took over $400,000 of the college fund that his wealthy landowner parents saved for his schooling and used it for the application for the Arousal Army. Even now his parents thought Oliver was traveling on a study abroad trip for school.

3: Marches and Formations

I am one of the last men to exit the locker room. I feel anonymous standing in a line of loincloth-clad shirtless men that extends to the left and right in a straight line stretching across the field. I stand at attention on my mark. I take in the large stage covered by a curtain in the middle of the stadium.

sissy Charlene is posing in front of the purple velvet curtain and holding a hot pink megaphone with rhinestones. Her blonde pigtails contrast with the dark curtain behind her, and her white platform Mary Janes shine under the stage lights. A slight breeze reveals the caged cock underneath sissy Charlene's sheer flouncy skirt. sissy Charlene also has on a male corset that has been pulled tight over an off-the-shoulder white blouse. Her make-up features thick black cat-eye eyeliner and bright pink lipstick. sissy Charlene also has false eyelashes that she bats dramatically in between announcements. I can't help but wonder how the 6'4" man is able to walk in his six-inch platform heels. The bright white Mary Janes look very campy.

"All right, boys," sissy Charlene shouts. "There are a few basics you need to know if you are going to be successful here at Femdom Boot Camp."

"Yes, sissy Charlene," Oliver responds. His British accent makes him sound particularly refined.

"Good boy," sissy Charlene says, as she raised one perfectly plucked eyebrow. "You'll move up quickly in our ranks if you continue being so obedient. This young fellow just showed you older men what to do! Whenever a Mistress or one of her sissies gives you a command, you must repeat, 'Yes, Mistress,' or 'Yes, sissy.' New Recruits, do you understand?"

"Yes, sissy," the swarm of loincloth-clad men chant in unison.

"Perfect, boys," sissy Charlene says and laughs with glee. "Next, you need to learn the salute. Whenever you hear this whistle—" she pauses to blow a high tweeting sound in the shiny silver whistle that is hanging around her neck. "At the sound of this whistle, salute your sissy guides and the Mistresses as so," sissy Charlene says. She moves her right hand to her forehead and holds her gloved hand over her brow in salute.

"Yes, sissy," a few men bellow. I can easily make out Oliver's goody-two-shoes British accent.

"Er, yes, sissy!" I quickly shout, hoping that no one will notice I chimed in a bit late.

Immediately, I feel the pop of a leather riding crop against my bare ass. "Ouch!" I shout, and leap in the air. I turn around and see sissy maid Rita brandishing the crop.

"What do you say?" sissy Rita asks.

"Thank you, sissy," I say, embarrassed. My cheeks (both those on my face and my butt) are flushed red and feel warm.

At that moment, a loud whistle rings out from the stage. I look up at the elevated platform and see Mistress Insomnia, the beautiful woman with dark hair and pale skin whose face was in the ad in *Kinky Times*. She is clad from head to toe in black leather and is making announcements from a sparkling megaphone that appears to be bedazzled with rhinestones.

"Welcome to Femdom Boot Camp, New Recruits. Here the Mistresses are in charge, and, of course, we reserve the full right to eject any man from the stadium at any moment," she notes. "Rest assured that you will be unlocked from your cage by the key holder submissives if you are not selected or if you choose not to continue."

I feel completely disposable and more than slightly intimidated, but it is a relief at least to know I won't be stuck in the cage forever even if I am ejected from the experience.

"We fully respect your informed consent, and we recognize that you have the right to revoke your consent at any moment, no matter what," the beautiful Mistress Insomnia continues. "BUT we are not all mind readers, so you have to speak up when you are uncomfortable."

"Yes, Mistress," the men echo.

"Safe words may vary based on the type of play," Mistress Insomnia continues. "You will be instructed on what to do in different scenarios, such as bondage, sensory deprivation, wearing a gag, and more as you advance in Boot Camp. Tonight, it is most important to know if at any time you want to stop immediately, say or shout, 'Red.' If you feel uncomfortable, but do not want to stop, say or shout, 'Yellow.' And if you really enjoy something and do not want it to stop, you can say, 'Green.'"

"But beware, some of us are sadistic and may not respond the way you'd hope when you tell us you do or don't like something," she says, then winks and cackles.

I feel extremely anxious. I am definitely less physically impressive than many of the men on the field, but the Mistresses are even more beautiful than I'd imagined. It isn't just their physical beauty and sexy feminine bodies that draw me in. It is also their presence.

Mistress Insomnia's chilly demeanor turns me on. She emanates strength and power, and this arouses my lust. I feel my dick growing inside my cold steel cage whenever I look at her in her full-body leather catsuit. I can't help but imagine what it would be like to be her slave. How would she treat me? What would she expect of me? What would she have me do?

For now, imagining is all Oliver, the 18-year-old British lad, can do—he has not even lost his virginity yet, though he's spent more hours than he'd care to count watching femdom porn on the internet. Oliver hasn't found a woman he thinks he can share his desires with, so he hasn't even bothered trying with anyone he's met. He had one high school girlfriend he left at home when he went to college. She was sweet, but far too innocent to understand his deeper desires.

Oliver remembered the first time he had kissed her with tongue. She kind of jerked back and jumped up in shock. "What was that?" she asked him.

"It's called a French kiss," he told her.

"Let's not do that anymore," she said. They stuck with closed mouth kissing from that point forward. When Oliver kissed her, she'd stand as stiff as a board. It seemed impossible to get her to relax. One time he'd tried massaging her shoulders, and she stayed so tense, he started to wonder if he was doing something wrong and hurting her.

Oliver's girlfriend been brought up in a very conservative Baptist family and raised to believe sex was sinful. Even though she was a loving and kind girl, she never exhibited any sexual desire towards Oliver. They dated for two years, and he had never even seen her without a shirt on. It had actually started to affect Oliver's confidence, because he hadn't had much experience, and he wasn't sure how much of her lackluster response was due to her upbringing, and how much was due to his skill level or lack of charm.

Now, Oliver is standing on the 50-yard line and trying to stop his legs from shaking. He feels like he was about to wet himself, even though he used the bathroom before the cock cage fitting. Oliver is next to Fred, the extremely tall and extremely athletic African-American man I'd met in the limousine. Even though he has sculpted arm and leg muscles, Fred Johnson has a bit of a pudgy gut, and his short-shaven hair is dappled with gray.

I couldn't help but wonder how old the dude is, but

I didn't dare ask. I saw Mistress Insomnia get on to the man earlier for whispering. I know the Mistresses valued obedience above all else, and I am here to please them—not any of the men. I do not want to mess up my chances now.

"Left, left. Left, right, left. Left, left. Left, right, left," shouts Mistress Doom through her sparkly megaphone. The petite and curvy Mistress has a slight Southern drawl when she commands, "Step in line, boys!" The men are now marching in formation around Mile High Stadium. The Mistresses made us form various shapes and were training us how to move across the field together. It is honestly pretty confusing trying to keep up with the movements while maintaining my spot in the formation. If anyone misses a step, Mistress Intrigue is quick to shout humiliating insults through her megaphone.

"Move faster, you maggots!" she snarls. "You are lowlier than the crust that forms between your stinky toes and hairy asscracks!"

No one's ever talked to me like that before, and I fee ashamed and slightly emotionally upset. Again, I have the nagging thought, *Why did I answer that ad?*

Suddenly I feel a sharp stinging sensation on my ass. I look up and Mistress Doom smiles. Her luscious, sexy cleavage pours out of her catsuit. "Pay attention, plebe!" she says. "Don't get lost in your thoughts." Mistress Doom hits my exposed butt with a leather riding crop as I marched. A bright pink spot forms on my butt cheek. Suddenly my attention returns to the present moment. I hadn't realized I had been so distracted in thought, but now I realize I had been lost in my head.

"Y-y-yes, Mistress," I say softly.

"What was that, boy?" she shouts.

"Yes, Mistress!"

"Good boy," Mistress Doom says. She stops in her tracks, swivels on her lace-up, knee-high leather boots, and turns to face me. She wraps her long, elegant fingers under my chin and raises my face so I am looking her straight in the eye. I can feel her cat claw fingernails digging into my jaw. "You'd be a better boy if you'd stay present and pay attention to your Mistress, though," Mistress Doom adds.

Mistress Doom lets go of my chin and shouts into the microphone again. "Left, left, left, right, left." The formation of around 100 faceless, nameless men continues to march around the stadium.

At this point, the Mistresses have rejected several men from Femdom Boot Camp for basic insubordination or slowness at following orders. I wonder how many of us remain. We are in a solid block of ten by nine men, with three leading on their own line in front of the others. Maybe there are 93 of us left?

I notice that one of the leaders is Leonard, the guy with the diamond earrings I'd met in the limo from the airport. *I wonder why the Mistresses picked that guy as one of the leaders…* I thought. *And why they didn't pick me…* My gaze fell to my rotund belly. I noticed that the trail of dark unruly hair on my belly stood out against my pale skin (and not in a good way). I looked ghastly white, like I hadn't seen a bit of sun in years.

If you think the surface level is unappealing, what do you think of this? Mistress Insomnia's voice suddenly cut through my thoughts, and I had a flash of myself vomiting on my sexual partner in the airplane bathroom.

What the…? I couldn't quite place the memory. *Did that actually happen?* I thought about how badly my pants had smelled when I woke up and remembered how the woman across the aisle had consciously averted eye and avoided me.

I fought the feeling of anxiety that gripped my stomach. I had a sinking feeling that I had been a very naughty boy last night, and that I'd had so much to drink that I didn't even remember what I had done.

How could she even know that? Did this woman have super powers? I was familiar with the theory of female superiority due to my dalliance with women's studies courses in college. The theory posits that women are naturally dominant to men and are superior in every way. Adherents point to evidence such as women's longer lifespans, ability to bear and nourish children, higher pain tolerance, multi-tasking ability, relational and emotional intelligence, physical beauty and charm, and psychic and intuitive wisdom. I wonder if it might be true, because this woman clearly has super powers.

Extremists take the theory of female superiority to the extent of wanting to establish a society completely free of men, as with radical lesbian separatism. Modern science is making these dreams seem more probable; lab-based impregnation techniques might make it possible for a woman to become pregnant without needing a man to even provide the sperm. In this way, some female thought-leaders see a path to create a new world that is free from patriarchal control and misogyny.

Whatever is going on with Mistress Insomnia and my thoughts, it is pretty weird. I peek out of the corner of my eye and notice Quinn marching next to me. Quinn's head is hanging down, and it seems like his legs are moving almost robotically. Was my friend OK?

I don't have much time to think before I feel another stinging sensation on my bare ass. "Ouch!" I shout, as I jump, and my hands instinctively rub the freshly spanked spot.

Mistress Doom runs over and grabs me by the ear. I can hear her tall boots pounding on the Astroturf as she darts over. "Ouch!!!" I shout, even louder this time, as pain radiates around her pinch.

"Submissives are to be seen and not heard," Mistress Insomnia instructs from up ahead. "And I can hear your whining all the way on the 25-yard line!"

Mistress Doom drags me by the ear up on to the stage. I almost lose control over my feet as I clumsily stumble up the stairs onto the dais. I feel extremely embarrassed standing in my tiny suede loincloth in front of all of the men, most of whom are still marching. A few of them have stopped moving in formation and are simply staring, waiting to see what Mistress Doom will do.

I feel a warm, wet sensation on my leg. I realize I am wetting myself out of nervousness. I look around, as if trying to find assistance, and realize I am alone. I want to cry. I feel completely and totally disgusting.

My hairy beer belly hangs down over the tan

loincloth, and the back flap barely covers my equally hairy ass crack. Sweat is dripping off my forehead, down my chest, over my protruding belly, and down off my balls. A tear runs down my cheek.

My once-mighty cock has shriveled in the cold chastity cage, and sweat mixes with urine and drips down my shrunken shaft and off the tip of my dick, then out the small hole at the tip of the device. I feel heat fill my face as I blush with shame and hope no one notices the wet rivulets running down my legs. I definitely have no way to hide my accident other than a divine miracle. I quickly think, *God, please, save me. Surely all those 'Hail Mary' prayers got me some of your good graces. Please, God, help me!*

I feel guilty for a moment and realize, part of me isn't sure if the Christian God would even accept me anymore. I'd dropped Catholicism by the time I got to college, mainly because I had opened more to Eastern spirituality after taking some Buddhist philosophy classes at NYU. I thought I'd gotten rid of my Catholic guilt a long time ago, but maybe not. My thoughts continue to race.

I snap back to reality when I hear Mistress Insomnia call sharply, "Boy, over here!" I look up and notice the leather-clad Mistress is standing by a wooden pillory up on stage. How had I not noticed that before?

I start to come to my senses and remember to shout obediently and loudly, "Yes, Mistress!"

The pillory has been set up on the stage with a spotlight shining on it. It was night time when we arrived, and now the stars have come out. There is a tiny sliver of a crescent moon. The stadium lights flood the field with bright white light. The spotlight is even stronger, though, so I figure no one will miss a moment of the punishment that is about to take place.

"Return to your yard lines, New Recruits," Mistress Intrigue commands through her megaphone. The rest of the men abandon their geometric formation drills and go back to their assigned yard lines, where they stand at attention and look at the Mistresses, who have all returned to the stage.

"Watch and learn, you worms," Mistress Doom shouts. Her bright marigold-colored hair seems to glow underneath the stage lights.

"Yes, Mistress," the New Recruits holler back. Our voices echo in unison off the walls of the stadium, and it sounds like there are hundreds of us instead of just around 100.

Mistress Intrigue helps me place my wrists in the rough wooden holes of the pillory, and she guides my head into the larger center hole before closing the plank over the top of the pillory and latching it shut. I get a good view of her stiletto boots as she works on the device.

"Bend over, boy," she says. I stick my butt out. I am acutely aware of the loincloth flap that barely covers my ass and the stifling metal cage encasing my cock. Again, I have the thought: *Why did I answer that ad?*

"Ouch!" I shout and leap into the air.

"You mean, 'Yes, Mistress!'" sissy Charlene shouts from the side of the stage. I can't see the sissy maid because I can't turn my head, but I recognize the voice.

"Yes, Mistress!" I bark.

"Good boy," Mistress Intrigue said. Her long black hair is blowing in the wind, and I think her pert breasts look stunning through the tight leather bodice of her catsuit.

Mistress Insomnia notices me eyeing Mistress Intrigue up and down. "Here, men are the objects, and you clearly still need a lot of training," Mistress Insomnia replies.

"That's for sure," Mistress Doom laughs, and spanks me hard, with her wooden paddle. My rear end aches at the impact. I feel tears come to my eyes.

I can't believe the feeling of shame.

Suddenly, I have a flashback to a childhood memory, when my dad spanked me for stealing something from a store.

We had stopped at a gas station to fill up on a road trip, and I was drawn to the candy aisle. I was about 10 at the time. I remembered seeing a Mr. Goodbar and, thinking my health-nut adoptive father wouldn't buy it even if I had asked, I shoved the candy bar in my pocket. My dad noticed that I was walking strangely and realized I was trying to take the candy bar. He pulled the candy out of my pocket and publicly chastised me outside the gas station. He spanked me hard publicly and told me that greed was sinful and the devil made me steal. The sensation of being spanked brought me back there for a moment.

"Ouch!" I shout again. Mistress Doom spanks me hard with the paddle, and my legs jump into the air without my conscious awareness. My butt stings from the momentum of the paddle.

Mistress Doom grabs my ear and says, "What do

you say, boy?"

"Y-y-yes, Mistress," I stutter. I feel my hand try to move to scratch my arm with a nervous tic, but it can't, because I was bound in the pillory.

"Say it again," Mistress Insomnia shouts. She cracks her riding crop against her leather gloved hand.

"Yes, Mistress," I sigh.

"Good boy," Mistress Insomnia says. She joins the others on the stage, but is still monitoring the men, who have returned to marching in formation. I am amazed to see the hordes of men march in sync, even without direction. The New Recruits are taking their training well. But I am feeling deeply insecure, and, honestly, it is painful. I am not sure what stings more at this point—my ego or my ass. Another tear falls down my cheek. Again comes the thought, *Why did I answer that ad?*

"You know why," Mistress Insomnia's voice arises in my mind. I can see her lithe leather-clad form out of the corner of my eye. I watch her shiny, pointy boots move closer to me, and I hear them clack across the wooden stage. Since my head is bound in the pillory, I can't look her in the eye. All I see is Mistress Insomnia's sharp pointy stiletto heel boots and the outline of her calves in her fitted leather catsuit. Mistress Insomnia crouches down, looks me in the eye, and winks. Her ice blue eyes meet my own, and I feel a tremor of recognition shoot up and down my

spine.

I normally would have nervously wrung my hands. Now I feel close to wetting myself yet again. My hands are bound, so I can't self-soothe in the habitual way. And I am acutely aware that the cadre of almost 100 men are now on the other side of the stage.

As he marches, Quinn glances up and catches a view of Theodore's pale white ass lifted high up in the air as his hands and head are bound in the pillory. Quinn giggles nervously at the sight.

"Left. Left. Left, right, left," Mistress Intrigue takes up the cry and interrupts Quinn's moment of mirth. The slender former model cracks her flogger against her thigh, and the sound echoes off the stage. The rest of the men continue to march, as Mistress Doom begins punishing a few more who have fallen behind. Her breasts bounce with each impact she makes with the wooden paddle.

A stocky man with golden, sun-kissed skin is panting and bent over, resting his hands on his knees when Mistress Doom grabs his ear. "Did we tell you to stop, boy?"

"No, Mistress!" Kahua Kahale responds. His feet scramble to keep up as Mistress Doom drags him onto the stage. She runs her sharp golden fingernails over his strong barrel chest before she bends him over roughly and places his head and hands into another pillory on the stage beside me.

Kahua wishes the pillory cuffs were lined with something soft, like velvet or fur. Instead, his wrists rest on rough-hewn wood, and Kahua even feels like he has a few splinters stuck in his arms. Of course, he can't get them out now—or for the foreseeable future.

But Kahua doesn't mind. A successful resort hotel chain owner and operator in Hawaii, he has a failed marriage and two teenage kids still on the island. At age 54, Kahua still hasn't found love. Although he is a bit of a hopeless romantic, what Kahua longs for more than love is deep submission to a powerful Mistress.

Kahua had answered the ad in *Kinky Times* without hesitation. And even though he is slightly humiliated to be bound in the pillory, it is all worth it for the sweet feeling of submission that are filling his body, mind, heart, and soul.

"Tell me why you're in the pillory," Mistress Doom shouts.

"I couldn't keep up, Mistress."

"That's right, boy. You fell behind, and so you must be punished," she replies.

"Yes, Mistress," Kahua feels Mistress Doom's sharp nails rub across his bare back. She steps her fingers down his lower back before spanking him hard on the ass with her bare hand. Kahua can't help but jump up in the air at the feeling of the impact. He feels his dick pulsing as it grows hard but presses up against the stainless-steel cock ring. It fees painful. He wonders if his ring might be a bit too small. For now, he can handle it, but not for much longer…

Mistress Doom grabs a flogger from the wall of toys on the stage. The wall features whips, chains, handcuffs, floggers, ball gags, dildos, and more contraptions I am not familiar with.

"Bend over and stick your ass up even more, boy," Mistress Doom commands Kahua.

He closes his eyes, and presses his hips back so his ass is pointed high in the air. Kahua can feel a gentle breeze blow over his inner thighs, which are slightly damp from sweat under his loincloth.

"Yes, Mistress!"

"Now you are a good and obedient boy, aren't you?"

"Yes, Mistress!" Kahua shouts.

Mistress Doom flogs him, and with a gentle flick of her wrist, what seems like a low-impact sensation transforms into a sharp shot of pain. It is all Kahua can do not to jump into the air or squeal like a pig. He hunts wild pigs with his family in Hawaii, so he knows the sound well.

"Say, 'More, Mistress,'" Mistress Doom demands. She cracks the flogger against her palm.

"More, Mistress."

The leather flogger flicks again across his exposed rear end. Kahua's tan ass contrasts with my pale white booty. My butt looks like the butt of a sedentary office worker. Kahua's behind is round and strong.

That man must work out, thinks Oliver. The scrawny 18-year-old feels a bit embarrassed. He has no muscle. His arms look like toothpicks. In fact, Toothpick was Oliver's high school nickname.

Kahua, on the other hand, has arms of a man who can haul wood or carry a heavy load. He looks like a muscular super hero with his strong chest. Oliver looks down at his pasty concave chest. When had that curly chest hair grown there?

As he gets distracted, Mistress Intrigue calls Oliver out: "You! You're behind formation. Come on stage now."

"Yes, Mistress," Oliver shouts. He, too, feels as if he might wet himself out of anxiety.

"Get on your hands and knees, boy," Mistress Intrigue orders. Oliver eyes the zipper that runs alluringly from the front to back of her catsuit.

"What?" he asks.

"Don't ask questions!" Mistress Intrigue spanks

Oliver's bare ass. I can hear a loud thwap. "Get on the floor!" the Mistress orders, then whacks the young man's butt hard. "What do you say?"

"Yes, Mistress."

"Good, now do it! Talk is cheap!"

Oliver crouches down, then puts his weight on his hands and knees. Mistress Intrigue approaches him. He swears he can see the outline of a G-string through her tight catsuit. She lowers her leather-clad ass firmly onto his back.

"Stay still," she says. "I need a seat. You are an object to me." Meanwhile, the rest of the men continue to march in formation around the field. Every once in a while, I can see Quinn's head swivel to check out what is going on. A few other men glance up as well. Mistresses Intrigue and Mistress Doom are monitoring them and occasionally spanking one that falls out of line.

The women look amazing up on stage punishing the men. The latex on Mistress Intrigue shines next to the soft black leather catsuit on Mistress Doom. Mistress Intrigue is tall and slender, and Mistress Doom is short and Rubenesque. I thank my lucky stars that somehow I have ended up in the presence of these amazing goddesses.

Soon I have two friends on stage in the pillory with me, in addition to Kahua and Oliver. Leonard, the Hispanic man held in pillory on my right, stumbled while marching and accidentally fell, causing a bit of a pile-up among the other New Recruits. Leonard is 5′6″ and has slicked his hair back with some sort of gel that has rendered it immobile. He has a shiny gold diamond earring planted in his right ear. I am surprised that Charlene the sissy maid didn't make Leonard remove that during intake. They'd stripped me of my Rolex, and I feel a bit odd without my status symbol around my wrist.

Carl, the man on the pillory to the left, is balding and seems to be dozing off. I even hear him snore for a moment. The Mistresses pulled Carl out of the line when he turned right, rather than left, as directed. *Damn, these women are tough,* I think. *And this is still Day 1! What on earth would be next?*

4: Standing at Attention

After about an hour, Mistress Insomnia frees her captives from the pillory and releases the dozens of men who have piled up on stage. I notice many of the New Recruits are covered in sweat, and many have red marks that formed on their arms and neck since they were placed in the pillory for so long.

"Get back to your yard line in the original line formation and sit down," Mistress Insomnia instructs coldly through her diamond-encrusted megaphone. She towers over us standing on stage in her six-inch platform heels and full-body leather catsuit.

"Yes, ma'am," the men shout in unison as we hustle to our spots. Leonard looks at his dog tag to remember his line, and Oliver high-tails it to his spot. I shuffle to my mark and rub my butt, which is a bit tender from all the spankings I've received.

"Take a seat and relax for a moment," Mistress Intrigue directs the New Recruits. The slender Japanese goddess sits down on a beautiful gilded throne on stage next to Mistress Doom, who looks like an African queen, and Mistress Intrigue, the ice empress. It is the triple Goddess embodied on the stage, and I felt lucky to behold this beautiful sight. I wondered what might come next and what sorts of experiences I might have with these goddesses. Was I worthy to be in their presence? Only time—and their temperament—would tell.

I see sissy Charlene and sissy Rita enter the stadium. They have a water dispenser on wheels they are pushing past the line of men. sissy Charlene has on such high heels that I wonder how on earth she can push the cart. I notice my penis twitches a bit as sissy Charlene walks by. sissy Charlene looks really cute in the loose, fluffy sheer petticoat skirt she is wearing. *I wonder what is going on underneath the skirt...* I muse for a moment, then blush as I remember that I'd gotten hard during the fitting, and in front of all the other men!

Still, I do not mind being seen. In fact, I am a bit of an exhibitionist. But I feel a bit of shame that I'd been seen being aroused by a man. I chalk that up to my strict religious upbringing as well. I don't hate religion per se, but I hate a lot of things I've been taught under the guise of religion. And I have definitely been taught that two men having sex was—gasp—a sin.

But what does that even mean? As an adult, I often wrestle with the concept of sinfulness, which had constrained me so much in my childhood and youth. Whatever sin is, I know I am pushing the limits coming here to Femdom Boot Camp.

During college at NYU, I learned Buddhist meditation as part of a philosophy class. As I practiced meditation and became more aware of my thoughts, it was weird seeing how acculturated my mind was with social beliefs and standards that had nothing to do with my true desires, thoughts, or opinions.

For example, I myself see nothing wrong with same-sex relationships or just plain sexual encounters between two men or two women… or three men or three women… or two men and one woman… or three men and two women... The more the merrier, right?

Plus, I see nothing wrong with nonbinary people and transgender individuals enjoying sexual relationships of whatever kind they so choose, with whomever they chose, and in whatever combination they choose, and I know ultimately gender is a construct anyway...

I'm pretty open-minded, though I definitely have room to grow. I celebrate monogamy and polyamory, so long as either one is consensual. In this, I feel inspired by Victoria Woodhull, a suffragette who once ran for U.S. President. She scandalized feminists in 1871 with her statement that: "I am a free lover. I have an inalienable, constitutional and natural right to love whom I may, to love as long or short a period as I can; to change that love every day if I please."

It baffles me how much of human history boils down to authoritarian attempts to define, constrain, contort, or suppress real human sexual desire so that it might be "acceptable" to family, church, and state. *Maybe that's what sissy Rita got "liberation" from,* I think.

I suddenly leap into the air as I feel a hand gloved in leather touch my back unexpectedly. The beautiful, tall, and glamourous Mistress Intrigue unlocks the pillory and lets me out. She tosses her long locks over her shoulder. "New Recruit, come back to earth. You should be here in Denver at Mile High Stadium," calls Mistress Intrigue sharply. "Instead, you're lost in your head. Drop and give me 30."

"Y—y—yes, Mistress," I stammer. I wish I could impress her by dropping to the ground and doing a one-armed pushup with Kahua on my back, but I am not quite there today. I get my heart rate up making day trades and managing my hedge fund, but I don't have much time for cardio or weights at the gym, and it shows.

I manage to complete 30 push-ups, but the difficulty is clear by the strained expression on my face. I am embarrassed Quinn is watching me, and I also feel like some of the beefier athletic dudes are snickering. I am sure they see me shaking as I push my body weight up and down using my underdeveloped arms.

"Good job. Now back to your place," Mistress Insomnia says.

"Good job? You're being far too kind," Mistress Doom adds as she cracks a bullwhip ominously against the ground. "That was pathetic. This is Femdom Boot Camp, and we're not here to coddle you. You!" Mistress Doom turns her perfectly lined green eyes to gaze at me. The beautiful ebony goddess is extremely intimidating. I am currently shaking a bit in my loin cloth.

"Yes, Mistress?" I ask with a trembling voice. I feel scared and pretty unappealing at the moment. I reek of sweat from all of the formations, I am tired and hungover from the flight, plus I've peed myself and vomited all over myself since I left New Jersey.

It has to be at least midnight. I wonder when we will finally get our reprieve for the night. *They call me Mistress Insomnia,* the female voice intones in my thoughts. *Insomnia, Insomnia, Insomnia...* The voice echoes and repeats. *Gee, I really must be tired,* I think. Mistress Insomnia is staring right at me. I feel her gaze on my gut and simultaneously envision her eyes dancing in my mind. I feel like I am tripping, but I definitely didn't have time to visit a dispensary in Denver.

"Drop and do 30 more. And tomorrow morning, you get up at 5:30 A.M. for extra weight training in the gym. sissy Charlene will be your personal trainer, so don't be late."

"Yes, Mistress," I say.

"A few others need to report to early morning duty, based on your performance today," Mistress Doom continues through her megaphone. Mistresses Insomnia and Intrigue are seated on elaborate velvet thrones on the stage. Each dominatrix looks cool, calm, and collected in head-to-toe catsuits. Their nails are fabulous, and not a hair is out of place, despite having spent their evening relentlessly disciplining and punishing a cadre of around 100 grown men.

"We will be making cuts throughout the day tomorrow, so no one is safe. Always be on your best behavior," Mistress Doom continues. Her bright white teeth shine as she grins, and her bright green eyes flash with mischief as she winks at the New Recruits. "What do you say?"

"Yes, Mistress."

"That's right," Mistress Doom smiles. She rises from her throne and paces back and forth across the stage in her knee-high boots. I follow her curves as she walks and become mesmerized by her feminine form. "The following men will report for additional physical training tomorrow morning at 5:30 A.M.: yard lines 29N, 35N, 46N, 47N, 48S, 44S, 32S, 30S, 22S, 15S. We noticed you falling behind in today's formations and suggest you do extra cardio to strengthen your stamina," Mistress Doom says, and cracks her whip hard against the stage.

Oliver, the 18-year-old virgin, notices his lengthy cock gets hard at the sound of the whip. As it becomes erect, his penis chafes against the chastity cage. Oliver had his number called for additional physical exercise, so he'll consult with sissy Charlene first thing tomorrow about the fit for his chastity device.

It hurts a bit, but the pain isn't unbearable. And Oliver has a sentiment that for him, pain is more of a pleasure. After all, he now has a safe word, so what could go wrong? He is ready to break through all of his limitations to transform his rough spots into subservient tame traits. *Would his first time be as a sissy?* he wonders.

"Yes, Mistress," Oliver shouts along with the other men.

"Now, New Recruits, we will teach you the Boot Camp chant. Are you ready?" Mistress Intrigue asks. She has risen from her throne and is standing in front of the pillories up on stage. The stadium lights glint off the zipper that runs along the crotch of her catsuit.

"Yes, Mistress," the men obediently echo back. Not a single one hesitates or resists at this point. We speak totally in unison.

"You all are doing so well on your first night," Mistress Insomnia notes. She tosses her long, dark hair over her shoulder and smiles a sweet smile. "We are all quite pleased, so let's keep things this way."

"Yes, Mistress" the mob of men reply.

"Now stand up and shake your butts till I tell you to stop," Mistress Doom yells into the diamond-encrusted megaphone. "We want to see your dangle!"

The swarm of New Recruits stand up and begin shaking their hips and butts. I feel my cock dangling and jiggling, but the male chastity device fits snug and tight. I hear Fred say, "Oh no, Mistress, I need help!" My head swivels to take in the bulky man in his loincloth shaking his ass. The stainless-steel cock cage lies on the ground, and Fred's penis is hanging out free and uncaged. I can't help but notice his dick is smaller than mine by an inch or more.

"I see," Mistress Insomnia says. She is still sitting on the throne with her legs crossed. I love the view of the bottoms of her patent leather boots that I can see from the field. "sissy Charlene, please get our little pet here a smaller ring and fit it in front of the rest of the men."

"Yes, Mistress." sissy Charlene starts running in high heels to the locker room, presumably to get a smaller size ring.

Mistress Insomnia motions for Fred to climb up on stage and stand in the spotlight. She stands up on her platform heels, wheels a bondage cross up to a raised platform, and hooks Fred's arms into the red leather cuffs. "Yellow," Fred says.

"Ah, so you are uncomfortable?" asks Mistress Insomnia, and traces the leather of her riding crop across Fred's chest. "Can you withstand the discomfort, or do you need to go home?"

"I can handle it, I think, for you, Mistress. Please be gentle."

Mistress Insomnia slaps the leather of her riding crop against her gloved palm, and Fred flinches.

"You do NOT get to tell ME what to do," Mistress Insomnia yells, and slaps the side of his thigh with her crop.

"Yes, Mistress," Fred cries, a bit embarrassed and occupied with the stinging sensation on his thigh. He hadn't mean for it to be an order, but he can see how it sounds that way. Fred is at Femdom Boot Camp because he wants to purify himself of all the machismo and male privilege bullshit from society. How strange that, without conscious awareness, he keeps enacting it.

Fred is both anxious and turned on simultaneously. He is nervous because he deeply and truly wants to please the Mistresses. He hadn't meant to seem insubordinate with his comment. He is definitely not used to this power dynamic, but he likes what he sees.

As a star basketball player for the Chicago Bulls, Fred had no shortage of women throwing themselves at him after games and at team appearances. But he had always secretly desired a female-led relationship where his will was completely submissive to his woman's. He was too shy to tell his groupies about his true desires.

But now that Fred has retired, and now that he is growing older, Fred figures he might as well follow his heart before it is too late. He no longer cares what anyone thinks about his lifestyle choice. He feels he has to finally be free to be his true self, so Fred responded to the ad in *Kinky Times.*

In this moment, the buff former Chicago Bulls player is submerged in the sweet power of true submission. What once felt like a yellow has actually become a green after his conversation with Mistress Insomnia. For just a second, when Mistress smacks him with the crop, Fred loses all sense of identity. He experiences this momentary ego loss as if he is floating in a sweet blissful cloud.

Fred's arms pull gently against the cuffs. I eye the man's toned and bulky biceps and legs. Fred has toned washboard abs, and his arms and legs are extremely muscular. Plus, Fred's dark skin is smooth and clear from wrinkles. He has a smile that lights up his face, and Fred smiles often.

I can't help but compare my pale, pasty skin, which never sees the light of day, to Fred's flawless black complexion. I also nervously compare my protruding potbelly to Fred's tight abs. *How can a dude who's graying be more fit than I am?* I think jealously. I note my scrawny arms that spend days entering trades into a computer and find myself lacking when compared to this much-older man.

I never thought I had any issues, but at this point in Boot Camp, I start to feel extremely insecure. I am about to cry or scream if I don't get some sleep soon. And my belly is growling for some food. We've done a lot more physical activity than I am used to already. Not only have I been punished on stage, I've endured several different marching formations up and down the expansive football field at Mile High Stadium.

"I'm back!" sissy Charlene says. sissy Charlene prances over to the stage in her cute Mary Jane heels. She is holding a smaller stainless-steel cock ring between two manicured fingers. "Are you ready for me?"

"Yes, sissy Charlene," Fred says.

"Very good," Mistress Insomnia adds. "Now everyone stand at attention and watch. On the third sound of the whistle, I want everyone to be standing up straight and saluting. Use the special salute we taught you earlier."

"Yes, Mistress," the men echo back. I can't remember the salute, so I look around to catch Quinn's eye. Quinn notices me shrugging, so he flashes a quick, familiar hand motion. It was the one-in-the-pink, two-in-the-stink hand we'd both mastered during our time together in a fraternity at NYU. I could still remember some of Quinn's stories about that hand sign…

I hear three tweets of the whistle. I scramble to my feet and salute by bringing my hand to my forehead and pulling my ring finger into the palm with the thumb so that the pointer and middle finger and pinky point straight out. The other 100+ men do the same.

As they stand bare-chested in their loin cloths and watch the spotlighted bondage cross, sissy Charlene enters the stage, kneels down, and begins pulling Fred's cock and balls through the steel ring. Fred giggles slightly.

"I'm sorry," Fred says. "It just tickles."

"Did someone say tickle? Don't mind if I do," Mistress Intrigue says. Seemingly out of nowhere, she appears on stage with a feather tickler. Mistress Intrigue gleefully smiles as Fred twitches and twists with each flick of the feather against his skin.

"Stay still," she says.

"Yes, Mistress," he says. Fred feels the subtle sensations of the feathers against his skin and has to steel every nerve he has to resist responding to the tickling sensations. He uses his capacity to get in the flow to detach from his natural reactions.

Fred had trained his mind well during his years with the Bulls, so he can change his state of mind practically at will. Plus, he is used to overcoming his physical resistance through the intense physical training he'd completed during his basketball career. Before too long, he did so well at resisting that Mistress Intrigue tired of tickling him.

"I got that on you just in time!" sissy Charlene says, while standing up and smoothing her frilly light pink petticoat. "Consciously you could resist the tickling, but unconsciously, your little friend responded."

Fred looks down and notices his penis stood erect now and pushed against the new chastity device. It is uncomfortable, but it doesn't hurt. "This feels much better," he says. "Thank you, sissy Charlene."

I for once feel I came out on top with the comparison to Fred. I note my erect cock is girthier than the older man's, and a tad bit longer as well. I hadn't seen everyone's full package yet, but I had caught a few glimpses here and there when the loincloths had flapped open, so I feel confident that my member at least helped put me in the top 50% of the men here.

Your little clitty means less to me than you'd think, Mistress Insomnia's voice arose in my thoughts again. I am beginning to feel sleep-deprived.

Fortunately, Mistress Doom grabs her megaphone and begins to wrap things up, stating, "OK, you little worms, it is finally time for bed. We have arranged for you to be housed at our private estate on the outskirts of town. Go back to the locker room and see one of the sissies to let you out of your chastity devices for the evening. You will only wear them during the day at Femdom Boot Camp training while you are getting used to them."

Mistress Insomnia continues, "If you have any fit problems, do let one of the sissies know. Then, change into your street clothes. You will be transported to your lodging in the same groups that came here from the airport, so form a group out front and wait for your vehicles."

"Yes, Mistress," the men intone.

"You will be able to sleep in a bit because we know it has been a tough first day, and we have some surprises in store for you tomorrow..." she mysteriously cackles.

What does that mean? I wonder.

"Be ready for breakfast to be served in the lobby of your housing at 10 A.M. Your vehicle will leave to return to Mile High Stadium at 11 A.M. promptly. Do not miss your ride or breakfast because you won't get a second chance for either," Mistress Insomnia says through her diamond-encrusted megaphone.

"Yes, Mistress," the men respond. I catch Quinn's eye again and try to read his facial expression. He looks both amused and dazed. I figure he is probably a bit tired from the day of physical work and wonder how he feels about being suddenly stripped down and caged like that. I haven't yet processed what has happened and have a variety of complex emotions arising. I hope I can connect for a deeper conversation with Quinn in our living space since I trust him.

For now, I head silently back to the locker room, strip off my loincloth, and put on some slacks with a button-up shirt. It almost feels odd wearing clothing after being so bare all day long.

"Hey, man," Kahua greets me as he leaves the locker room. Kahua is with Oliver and a few of the other men I met before. "What'd you think about your first day?"

"Well, I definitely wasn't bored," I say, "But sometimes it was a bit uncomfortable."

"A bit?" Kahua hoots and laughs. "That was beyond the boundaries of my comfort zone for sure. But I loved it!" His tummy jiggles a bit as he laughs, and his eyes light up. *He has a great smile,* I think.

"You know, I think I loved it, too," I say. "The rush of submission felt unlike any drug I've ever tried—and honestly, I've tried a few. I am willing to do almost anything—and even be demeaned by these women—to get that feeling again."

"Hey man, that's cool," Kahua says. "And I mean, being demeaned by women? I might be weird, but I really get turned on by that. Ordinarily, I'm the head honcho in all my business dealings, and it feels great to be put in my place by these powerful dames."

Kahua turns toward the stadium, where a few men are still coming out of the locker room. "Guys, let's load up!" The men get into the limo. Everyone looks so different in their street clothes. Now I can practically picture everyone naked... And I notice thinking of Billy Button makes my cock begin to become erect. Now, there is none of the tightness and extra tension from the chastity cage, so my pants rise up as I become fully hard.

The driver shuts the door to the limo and starts the car. As the luxury vehicle heads to our lodging, I wonder what tomorrow will bring, and where we are headed for the night...

5: Good Night and Sweet Dreams

The car winds through the lamplit streets of Denver, and the driver takes 6th Avenue to the highway, then exits near Golden Gate Canyon Road. After a few miles, the line of limos passes a street sign that reads "Crawford Gulch."

I feel like I am far from the city out here, even though the drive has just been about 20 minutes. I enjoy gazing out of the sunroof during the drive. Hundreds of stars are sparkling in the night's sky; I have never seen so many stars in New York City or the New Jersey suburb where I live.

After a moment, the limos turn into a driveway and the drivers enter a code into the gate. A daunting iron gate with golden spikes springs into motion and cranks open to allow the limos access to the estate.

"What you see here is known as the Pleasure Palace," the driver tells the men. "And in case you are wondering, the answer is no. Out here, no one can hear you scream—or moan...especially once you're fitted with your ball gags!"

I gulp. *Am I really ready for all of this?* I think. I feel a little nervous and notice the sensation of a cold sweat forming on my balls. I am physically exhausted and my muscles are sore from the marching formations. I have also been through a roller coaster of emotions.

"Happy we survived our first day, man," Quinn says and smiles.

"For sure, dude," I reply.

The other men are craning their necks to get a glimpse of the Femdom Mansion through the heavily tinted limousine windows. After a 10-minute winding drive past tall evergreen trees, a beautiful white Mediterranean villa emerges. The men gasp at the awe-inspiring sight of the city of Denver lit up in the distance behind the mansion.

"I am ready for bed," I say.

"I wonder where we're sleeping," Quinn adds. At this point, it seems to be at least 2 or 3 A.M. The car pulls to a stop at a winding roundabout driveway and parks. There is a line of six or seven limos outside the house.

"Go ahead and get out. We delivered your luggage here after we picked you up at the airport. You'll find it's already stored next to your bed. Sweet dreams, and welcome to Golden, Colorado. The Mistresses own several hundred acres, and this is their Pleasure Palace," the driver chuckles knowingly. "Soon, they might just own you." He smiles. I wonder what the driver has seen in his time employed by the

Mistresses.

I notice two middle-aged men in gimp masks kneeling on all fours by the front door of the beautiful multi-story villa. Mistress Intrigue holds the leash for one man, who is naked except for his spiked leather collar and a spiked penis cage fastened around his mid-sized dick.

"Sit, bitch," Mistress Intrigue dictates, then smacks the faceless gimp's bare ass with her riding crop. The man drops his butt to the ground like a well-trained dog. "Good boy. You've earned this treat," Mistress Intrigue coos. She unzips the crotch of her leather catsuit and grabs the gimp's head. She shoves his mouth into her pussy and moans. "Lick it, my bitch. Lick my pussy like a good boy." She continues to smack her submissive's ass with the crop as he pleasures her.

In the meantime, Mistress Doom holds the leash of the other scrawny, dark-skinned gimp. She is watching Mistress Intrigue and getting wet. Mistress Doom yanks on the chain, grabs the gimp's collar, and guides his tongue to her pussy, which she reveals with a quick unzipping of her catsuit crotch. I hadn't noticed the zipper before because it blended in with the coloring of her leather bodysuit.

At just that moment, Kahua opens the door, and he

and Oliver are the first ones out of the car. "Feels good to be here," Oliver shouts. "This is heaps cooler than my flat back in London." Oliver still hasn't noticed the gimps worshipping the Mistresses' pussies, but Kahua is frozen in place like a deer caught in the headlights. I giggle a bit nervously.

The two leather-clad Mistresses are pressing their gimp's eager tongues and mouths into their exposed pussies. Kahua feels himself getting hard, but he isn't sure if he is allowed to come, and he doesn't want to find out by getting punished. It has been a long day, and he already has jet lag from flying in from Hawaii. So, he decides to play it cool.

Kahua opens the tall, heavy glass and gold door and holds it for the other men. "Thanks, buddy," I say. I wheel my bag inside and cross between the pair of Mistresses receiving oral pleasure from their gimps. I am so excited that I made it through my first day of basic training at Femdom Boot Camp and have arrived at the Pleasure Palace!

Oliver finally notices what is going on, and his jaw drops open. "Ohhhh... Uhh... Hi," he stammers before blushing and running inside and letting out a nervous giggle. "My mom would kill me if she knew what I was doing…" Oliver tells me.

"Dude, I forgot you were 18, but talking about your

freaking mom is a great reminder. It's time to grow up, buddy," I am talking with bravado to try to cover up how insecure I feel.

Neither Mistress Intrigue nor Mistress Doom seem to notice the New Recruits as we enter the house. Both women have taken a seat next to each other on a gilded iron bench by the front entrance. Mistress Doom is fully covered in leather, and latex hugs Mistress Intrigue's slender figure. The ladies are completely covered other than their unzipped crotches. The Mistresses toss their heads back and they are moaning as the gimps worship their pussies with their tongues.

I have a momentary flash of a fantasy. In my imagination, instead of ignoring me, Mistress Intrigue catches my eye, licks her lips, and says, "Come here, stud. I need that hard dick inside my tight pussy. I want to feel you inside me." Without realizing it, my hand creeps down to my penis to start some self-pleasure.

"Ouch! What the f—" I feel a sharp sensation on my balls as Mistress Doom flicks the tip of her long leather whip in my direction. She has expertly managed to inflict maximum pain on the soft tender spot on my scrotum. "Hands off my property, you little worm," she shouts. "You exist for my pleasure, not to pleasure yourself. Did you hear that, submissives? Hands off your little clitties from here on out!"

Feeling slightly ashamed, I shout, "Yes, Mistress!" I take one last sidelong look at the erotic display and shuffle inside before I get into more trouble. My balls still sting a little. Inside the Femdom Mansion is dazzling light and pristine white and black marble, with lots of mirrors, hallways—

And hidden passages. Another random thought arises in my mind, and it sounds like Mistress Insomnia's stern voice. I shake my head as if to wake up. *I may look like a dream, but I'm your worst nightmare,* the voice echoes in my thoughts.

"Sweet dreams, everyone. Your room is right down this hallway," a butler motions down a narrow hall at the back of the grand entry. The butler is clad in a black suit with white gloves and looks like a classic gentleman.

The room for the New Recruits to sleep in is a giant ballroom with a polished herringbone wooden dance floor. It has high ceilings and features gilded borders and columns. There is a luxurious and soft deep red carpet surrounding the dance floor. There is also an extremely tall stripper pole and a metal frame scaffold set up around the dance floor. Mirrors surround the pole on every side and reflect back the crew of New Recruits as we enter the room.

Dozens of Army cots have been placed evenly

around the room, and each cot has a rough burlap sleeping bag along with a thin-weave khaki blanket on top. The room is lit by dimmed chandeliers and wall votive candelabras. I spot my luggage next to a cot and sit down. Quinn's luggage is right next to mine. "Hey, Quinn, you're over here!" I call out.

Quinn smiles and heads over. "Long day, huh?" he says.

"The bathroom facilities are next to the main entry hall. Do make yourselves at home," a sissy slave remarks. I had not even noticed the sissy, who is serving as a human table with a tea set placed on his back. "And do help yourself to some tea," it says.

The sissy has a British accent and a mustache. It is on its hands and knees wearing a sheer fluffy white skirt with its cock sealed into a plastic cage that dangles between its legs.

"I'd like some tea, all right… some Long Island Iced Tea," I joke and wink at Quinn.

Quinn smiles and whispers into my ear: "Funny you should say that. I've got some hard liquor we can spike it with in my bag. Get us some cups and we can sneak to the bathroom together."

I smile knowingly and approach the sissy slave. "Thank you for the tea, kind sissy."

"Please don't call me any name," the sissy slave says. "I am only the Mistresses property and have no identity of my own. But do enjoy your tea." I ponder what I just heard while I pour tea and fill two porcelain cups with the lemon chamomile blend.

"Smells delightful," the sissy slave says. "Enjoy your tea."

"Thank you," I reply.

I subtly motion to Quinn, and the two of us head toward the bathrooms in a long, dark hall separate from the ballroom. Most of the men are settling into their cots and unpacking their belongings, and no one is near the lavatories. There is a bathroom at the end of the hallway that is a handicapped room with extra space, so we sneak into that one and lock the door. Quinn giggles and pulls out a travel bag filled with vodka, gin, tequila, rum, and triple sec.

"Damn, man, you know how to travel in style!" I cheer as Quinn pours the mini bottles into the tea.

"Cheers!" Quinn whispers and chugs his "Long Island" tea. "Let's be quiet so we don't get in trouble."

"Cheers! For sure," I say. "We already got in trouble once." I tip my head back and gulp the concoction. "So, what do you think of… all this?" I ask as the alcoholic brew trickles down my throat. I feel a fire burning down into my belly.

"Well, I'm not totally sure yet. Some of it's hot; some of it's scary. What do you think?" Quinn asks.

"I'm not sure what to make of it either. Are we

going to end up as sex slaves or sissies? I'm not sure if I have what it takes, and I think my balls are chafing. I'm also super tired," I sigh.

"My balls are chafing, too, man. Can you check them out? They gave us some Aqua Lube we can apply if they're chafed," Quinn says. I suddenly notice Quinn's curly hair and chiseled jawline. My friend is ripped, too. Quinn pulls down his boxers to show me the sore spots. He sits on the toilet and leans back so his luscious 9-inch cock dangles in the air.

I bend down to check it out. I hadn't realized my college buddy is so well-endowed! Quinn's penis has a lengthy shaft, but it is a bit on the thin side; his dick is tall and lanky, just like Quinn. I smell the musky aroma from my friend's nether regions and notice I start to feel a bit turned on, and my cock hardens. "I see some redness here," I say. "Can you check on me?" I catch Quinn's eye, then motion toward my now-hardening cock.

Quinn takes in my fat, bulging member. "Does that hurt after being in the cage all day? I do see some redness on you, too."

"It is a little painful, but it also feels kind of pleasurable. You know what I mean?" I ask.

Quinn gulps, blushing. He's never seen this lustful look in my eye before. My cock is turning reddish purple as the blood flows into it, and Quinn notices it is turning him on. He grabs the Aqua Lube and starts massaging it where the ring rubbed my balls raw. I moan gently, then grab the Aqua Lube and rub it onto Quinn's balls. The alcohol from our Long Island Iced Teas fills our bellies, and the two of us moan softly for a minute as we stroke each other.

"Can I lube up your asshole?" I ask Quinn. "I'd love to pleasure you with my finger."

Quinn feels an electric spark flash from his loins throughout his body. He's never been with a man before, but in this moment, he is so horny, he can't say no. Plus, he trusts me since I've been a good friend for years. Quinn has had a few lovers since his painful divorce, but he has found most of his relationships short-lived and unsatisfying. His last one-night-stand left him in the middle of the night without so much as a goodbye note. Quinn had grown bored of his nightly masturbation routine.

"Sure," he says. "Teach me how to pleasure you, too. Let's give each other some needed attention." I can't believe what is happening. Quinn hands me the vodka handle, and we each chug a bit more before turning to one another and grabbing each other's dicks.

Quinn excitedly pumps his hand up and down my hard shaft. It feels odd to be free after being caged all day. For a moment, I consider what it would feel like to be completely caged full-time. I heard it could be a blissful experience, but I also had been warned the life of chastity at the hands of a key holder was not easy. *Would this be one of the last times I might be able to get hard whenever I want?* I think. I take another sip of vodka, then grab Quinn's long, thin member.

Quinn starts to groan. I am so turned on imagining the others potentially hearing us, and I am drunk enough that I think I might even enjoy feeling watched by others. I take a hard swig of the rum, then the gin, and then lower my head down so I can suck on Quinn's shaft. He thrusts his pulsing penis persistently into my open mouth.

I have never actually given a man head before this moment, but I am driven by some sort of instinct. The lack of inhibitions from the alcohol makes it so I no longer care if I make a fool of myself. My horny brain drives me forward. I gag and tears stream from my eyes as I open my throat to allow Quinn's lengthy member deeper inside my mouth. Even though it is my first time giving, I've learned a few tricks from receiving head. I use my hand to stroke Quinn's cock so that my mouth only has to handle a few inches of his dick at one time.

Quinn's moans and thrusting are driving me wild. If I weren't so drunk, I would have wondered how hooking up might affect our friendship. I also might have considered if I might impact my participation in the Femdom Boot Camp. But instead, vodka vapors fill my mind and I forget all about the vow of chastity clause I'd signed off on when I had completed the consent forms and waivers at the beginning of the Femdom Boot Camp.

In the meantime, my penis is throbbing with desire for Quinn. I want to penetrate him and to feel him penetrate me. I have always wanted to experiment with anal sex, but all of my girlfriends have been quite prudish in the bedroom.

Aside from the uptight college girlfriend who ghosted me, I'd dated two girls in high school. One, Darlene, refused to give me oral sex, and she also refused oral sex from me. Raised in a stricter Catholic Church than I had been, Darlene considered nonprocreative sex sinful and insisted on wearing promise rings and maintaining chastity till marriage. After five months of dating, 20 dinners out, 5 movies, and 2 concerts, I hadn't even been able to finger her or even touch her pubic area or breasts.

My next high school girlfriend went to prom with me and a few football games. She was a nice girl who loved dogs and chocolate, but she was raised in a conservative Christian family. It seemed so wasteful to have her be so chaste, because Monica was curvaceous and extremely sexy. I loved holding her hand and kissing her. She did actually let me see her naked a few times, and I even got to fondle her breasts and her clitoris. I never did get a finger into her vagina, though.

I finally lost my virginity in college. I had been too embarrassed to tell her it was my first time, but I was happy to finally get it over with. We dated throughout college, and she was nice enough, but at the end of the day, kind of bland, ordinary, and far from dominant…

"Theodore?" Quinn asks.

"Huh?" I jolt back to reality. Quinn's member is still in my mouth, but I've stopped sucking or licking it. I can smell alcohol from my own breath.

"Let me pleasure you now," he says. "Take a seat." He gestures to the toilet, which has a golden lid. He grabs a fluffy, luxurious hand towel and places it on top of the seat, so I have a place to sit. My 6-inch cock is totally hard. The delicate skin down there feels rubbed raw after the tough day at Femdom Boot Camp. By this point, it is almost certainly 2 A.M. or later.

Good boys go to bed on time so they can be well-rested to serve their Mistresses, a thought flashes through my mind, followed by a cackling laugh and a mental image of Mistress Insomnia, winking at me. She is clad in a black leather catsuit and tall leather boots, and she continually cracks a long-tail whip as she laughs wickedly. Am I hallucinating or what? I've heard of people seeing pink elephants after drinking too much, but I hadn't had that much, had I? I nervously bite my fingernails and notice I am filled with anxiety and some guilt after the odd thought. *Is it possible this Mistress is some sort of witch?*

While I am getting lost in my thoughts, Quinn kisses me once on the mouth with tongue, then gently kisses my chest and even my big belly as he works his way down to my groin. As Quinn lowers his head to my crotch, I play with his curly blonde hair, and I start to moan in anticipation. My eyes begin to roll back in my head as pleasure pulses through my body…

6: Locked in a Chastity Cage

The next thing I know, I hear the triumphant sound of a bugle playing "Reveille" from out in the hallway. "New Recruits, look alive! It's time to make your cots and get ready for today's Femdom Boot Camp training!" I hear the distinctive voice of sissy Charlene shouting through a megaphone. I feel hungover yet again. I crack open one eye to see what is going on.

What the...? Why am I in the bathroom? I feel the cold tile beneath me and look around at the toilet bowl. It seems I passed out right here on the floor in the bathroom. *Shit! Wasn't I supposed to do special morning calisthenics today?* I think nervously. *And these hungover mornings with memory loss are starting to worry me a little.*

I cannot remember whatsoever why or how I ended up here, but I can smell my breath because it reeks strongly of vodka and cum. *I'd better brush my teeth and get ready before anyone notices I'm missing,* I think.

Don't fool yourself, boy. Mistress Insomnia's voice fills my thoughts. *This house has eyes. We already know more about what happened than even you do!* Mistress

Insomnia's image fills my mind's eye, and I see her cackle menacingly. I start scratching my arm nervously and wonder if I will get into real trouble—or worse, get kicked out of Femdom Boot Camp. I didn't spend hundreds of thousands of dollars just to get sent home early.

I drag myself to my feet and notice I still feel a little unstable due to my hangover. The vodka slushes back and forth in my gut as I stand, and it is difficult to balance. I can already tell today will be a tough day at Femdom Boot Camp. So much physical effort and extreme submission are challenging under normal circumstances, but now... *How had I even gotten vodka? And where on earth are my clothes?*

I grab a nearby towel and wrap it tight around my waist. It looks a little crusty, but at this point, I know beggars most definitely cannot be choosers. This filthy used towel will just have to do until I can find my clothes.

I walk up to the ornate mirror and feel horrified at what greets me. I have dark circles under my eyes, and I look like I haven't slept in years. Without consciously intending to do so, I groan at my haggard appearance. I look and feel like I have been hit by a truck. I am a far cry from a *GQ* model.

I try to smooth down my hair, then quickly brush my teeth and rush outside. I can't even remember where my assigned cot is. Maybe Quinn can help me...?

I find Quinn next to a threadbare tan military cot spray-painted with a stenciled number 46N, which matches Quinn's yard line. Quinn is unpacking a camouflage duffle bag at the foot of the cot when I walk up. I feel my manhood harden as I approached Quinn. I am already getting tired of the feeling of my chafed skin, though I am still curious about what it will feel like to be fully caged and held at the whim of three powerful Mistresses long-term. I've read that living in full chastity in a female-led relationship can be a blissful experience that unleashes the feeling of complete and total erotic and spiritual submission.

I've been through Catholic school and never had any meaningful religious or spiritual experience. I fell asleep during Mass, was told I was sinful for having sexual urges, and was asked for money to support the ministry. After a while, I started to doubt the spiritual teachings from my childhood and parents' tradition.

For me, this Femdom Boot Camp is not just a sexual thing. I am truly seeking complete sexual and spiritual liberation while on earth. Still, at this point, I can't focus too much on my lofty ideals. Honestly, I am just surprised my body has the capacity to generate an erection, considering the massive hangover I have.

"How's it going?" Quinn asks and winks at me

flirtatiously.

I lean in and whisper, "I am super hungover. I woke up on the floor, and I don't even remember how I ended up in the bathroom. Do you know?"

Just at that moment, a piercing whistle blasts through the large ballroom that has been converted into a makeshift bedroom for the multitudes of New Recruits. Even though many men have been kicked out yesterday, about 90 or 100 still remain. At the sound of the whistle, each New Recruit instantly stands at attention next to his cot and salutes the stage platform that has been set up in the middle of the grand ballroom.

Mistress Intrigue is standing next to sissy Charlene on the platform. She is wearing leather hot pants that show off her long, lean legs. She also has a leather bikini top that is so small it barely covers her nipples. Even though she is almost entirely nude, I think she looks extremely sexy and powerful. She is holding a long, braided whip in one hand and a leash on the other.

sissy Charlene is in a sheer hot pink tutu. The stiff fabric points away from the hips so that the cock cage underneath is highlighted. Today, sissy Charlene also has on a tight and shiny hot pink long-sleeve top. I can see a bra-line underneath the shirt. I assume the bra is holding some sort of breast inserts that create the illusion of a full chest.

sissy Charlene must have been at least 50 years old.

She has wrinkles formed by the years around her eyes, which are made up with heavy eyeliner and eyeshadow. Her age also shows in laugh and frown lines by her mouth, which is painted on with hot pink lipstick. sissy Charlene shaves her legs and armpits bare. She is wearing short, light pinks socks with ruffles and shiny patent leather Mary Janes to complete her outfit.

Mistress Intrigue has connected a leather leash to a gilded collar that has been fastened tightly around sissy Charlene's throat. It does not appear that sissy Charlene minds the leash or the collar. In fact, it seems that sissy Charlene is really flattered by the attention.

As I take in the scene, out of nowhere, I feel a sharp pang on my chest. I am still wrapped in a crusty towel, but otherwise nude, and I still feel hungover and extremely disoriented. "What the heck?" I say, as I rub a now-tender part of my chest.

"Submissives are to be seen and not heard," Mistress Intrigue commands through her megaphone. She uses her long-tail whip to flick my chest all the way from the stage platform several feet away.

"Yes, Mistress," I say, and lower my eyes to the ground. I have a feeling that now she is going to make an example of me…

"Do you know why I punished you specifically, New Recruit?" she calls.

I feel kind of like a traffic officer had stopped me on the side of the highway and asked me, "Do you know why I pulled you over?" It is never a good idea to answer questions like that.

"No, m-m-ma'am," I stutter.

"Open your eyes and look around, New Recruit," she says, then whips me several more times across the chest. Her tiny titties almost pop out of her bikini top as she lashes me. Each lashing leaves a bright pink line across my chest, so it looks like I have a tender red X on my upper body. Her aim is astoundingly accurate, considering the fact that the stage is more than 8 feet away from me.

"Ouch!" I shout and double over. The pain radiates through my body, and when I look down, I see the large red welt across my chest. Before I can stand up, Mistress Intrigue delivers 10 more lashes across my upper back. My cock twitches when I hear the sound of the whip hitting my skin. Even though it is decidedly painful, something about it is also turning me on. I've never had a woman treat me this way before, and I have to admit, I really like it. I'm a bit of a masochist.

I look up at her face and notice Mistress Intrigue's mouth is twisted into a gleeful smile. She is sadistically enjoying my pain quite a bit. Although she is a classic Japanese beauty, there is something sinister about her. I feel like I am about to either puke or cry, and I don't want to do either one in front of the whole group.

"New Recruits, what do you say when a Mistress blesses you with a correction?" Mistress Intrigue asks through the microphone.

sissy Charlene and a few New Recruits, including Quinn, respond: "Thank you, Mistress."

"That's right, boys," Mistress Intrigue says.

"Y-y-yes, Mistress," I manage to mutter. At this point, I just want a continental breakfast and a cup of coffee. The sun isn't even up yet. It is probably 5 A.M. or even earlier. The booze is still sloshing around in my belly and bloodstream, and on top of it, I have to pee. My penis is pretty chafed, and I have no clue why I woke up in the bathroom or how I even got the alcohol to begin with! I do know alcohol is strictly prohibited, though, so I try to play it cool.

Mistress Intrigue walks off the stage and grabs me by the ear. I want to scream, as her pinch hurts me greatly, but I feel it is not befitting a New Recruit to openly express displeasure. I try to hold it in and submit to her will.

From the vantage point of the stage, I can see clearly why she is upset at me. Every other cot is fully made, and each New Recruit is standing obediently next to his cot, wearing his loincloth and saluting the stage as we'd been taught by sissy Charlene. Some of the men have oiled up their chest and arm muscles.

One dude is even flexing. These guys look like total beefcakes who are totally submissive. I look like I am pregnant because my fat gut is so big, and I am trying to cover myself with a towel that reeks of liquor and has crusty white marks on it.

As if my personal appearance isn't bad enough, I see what is presumably my cot, which is on the other side of the room and features messy, tangled sheets. There seems to be some sort of stains on them. I squint my eyes to see and think I might be seeing a combination of saliva, semen, vomit, and sweat on the sheets. The vomit probably reeks of alcohol. *What the hell did I do last night?* I wonder. I nervously itch my chin and glance at Quinn, who looks scared. He is no longer smiling.

My threadbare comforter is lying on the ground, and my suitcase is open with objects pouring out of it. I can see my loincloth hanging out of a suitcase pocket. It seems like the items I packed have been shuffled through. I am completely embarrassed. I look like a total slob and loser at this point.

"Ouch," I accidentally squeal when Mistress Intrigue stops pulling my ear and instead yanks hard on my cock to direct me toward my unkempt cot. I immediately feel a cold bucket of water dumped on my head from above. sissy Charlene has snuck up on me from behind and is using a champagne ice bucket to discipline me. It is definitely easier for her because she is in extremely high heels, which makes her tower over me at 7 feet tall.

I can't see anything because of the water in my eyes, and my nipples are hard. I can feel goose bumps form all over my body. The gunky towel is now soaking wet, and in my shock, I drop it on the ground. I hear at least a few men snickering as the icy liquid drips down over my head, soaking my hair and running down my body into the lush ballroom carpet.

"Look at that little clitty," Mistress Intrigue cackles. I crack open my eyes and see her smile brightly as she grabs a small studded leather cat-of-nine-tails from a utility belt around her waist. Without hesitation, Mistress Intrigue pops the cat-of-nine-tails against my penis. Several of the pointy studs hit my shaft hard.

My balls and shaft were pulled through the stainless-steel cock ring at the chastity cage fitting yesterday. My ring was probably a little too small, because my skin is chafed, and I am constantly aware of an uncomfortable feeling in my nether region. My balls look extra pink, and I can see a few places I'd missed when shaving.

I try to hold in my discontent as Mistress Intrigue continues to flail my sore, limp penis with her studded cat-of-nine-tails, but to my chagrin, a squeal of pain escapes from my lips. I feel like my dick has been hit by a bunch of tiny hammers, and the pain continues to radiate around my most sensitive zone.

I raise my head and look around the room. Quinn is averting his eyes as if he is ashamed on my behalf. Kahua is holding in laughter. I can see his big, round belly shaking with mirth, as he tries to keep a straight face. And scrawny young Oliver is standing with his mouth wide open in shock. Brandon is grimacing and looking at my red, throbbing member. Andrew won't meet my eye and is looking away from the scene.

"Submissives, every single one of you followed our instructions—except you, slug," Mistress Intrigue exclaims. "The rest of you can go to breakfast while we perform our inspection for contraband. But you—" she gestures at me "You must stay behind for punishment. sissy Charlene, prepare the cage."

"What the—?" I say, without thinking.

"Submissives are to be seen and not heard," Mistress Intrigue shouts, then shoves me towards a tall column in the corner covered by a velvet curtain. sissy Charlene pulls the curtain and reveals a golden wire cage. It is big enough for a giant dog, but the cage doesn't have enough room for a human to fully stand. sissy Charlene opens the door, and Mistress Intrigue smacks my balls, then pushes my head down so I double in half, and she guides me into the cage.

"How long will I have to be in here?" I shout. I feel like crying. The bars of the cage are digging into my naked legs and ass. I can't breathe very easily since I can't fully stand up, and now I realize I feel like I have to pee.

Mistress Intrigue just ignores me. I can smell eggs, bacon, and coffee wafting in from the dining hall. The sound of laughter and joy echoes into the room. I hear my stomach growl, and I try to hold in the stream of urine that threatens to release. I am packed into the cage in a very uncomfortable position, but I can see the entirety of the sleeping room.

sissy Charlene, sissy Rita, and Mistress Intrigue go methodically from cot to cot and open each New Recruit's luggage. Most bags are cleared, but they focus in on a select few items that they find in some of the suitcases.

sissy maid Charlene pulls out some lacy thongs from one young man's bags and throws them in a container for contraband. "Who does this one think he is?" sissy Charlene says. "New Recruits are not allowed fancy panties! The nerve!"

sissy Rita takes notes on a clipboard. I assume Rita is noting which New Recruits have infractions so that they can be punished.

After a round around the room, the container is filled with some panties, junk food, and other contraband that New Recruits smuggled in. One man brought some trashy porn magazines, and another had a Fleshlight.

"What are these men thinking?" Mistress Intrigue asks. "Did they even read the waiver they signed? Each man should know that no porn or masturbation is allowed during Femdom Bootcamp!"

As they approach my cot and luggage, I gulp. I feel really stupid. I never thought they would inspect what I packed, but I should have known. sissy Charlene pulls five pornographic magazines from my bag, as well as five or six empty miniature liquor bottles. I don't remember bringing those...

You wouldn't! The voice of Mistress Insomnia inexplicably fills my thoughts. *Do you even remember your own name?* The Mistresses also take my solid black butt plug for the duration of Femdom Boot Camp just in case I might get too much pleasure from wearing it. Of all the bags, mine definitely has the most contraband.

Mistress Intrigue suddenly pops up right by the side of the cage. "This is your bag?"

"Yes, Mistress."

"You will spend the morning in this cage and join us after lunch," she says coldly. The beautiful woman stands up and swivels on her stiletto heels, and then she and the two sissies turn off the lights and leave the ballroom. I am literally left in the dark. I can hear muffled laughter and chatter from outside. After a while, I can't hold my bladder any more, and urine sprays down my legs. I feel disgusting and humiliated.

Has it even been an hour yet? There are no windows or clocks, so I have no sense of time. Eventually I hear some shuffling, and the front door slams shut. I can make out the sound of the limousines starting up. The men must be heading to Mile High Stadium for the call time. I just want to cry. I am cold in this cage, and the bars are hurting my skin. My balls and cock are still chafed after being squeezed into that tiny cage yesterday, and I am covered in urine. On top of that, I feel like my blood is made of alcohol, and my stomach keeps growling. Would I ever make it back from this?

7: The Youngest New Recruit

After several hours that feel like days, sissy Charlene returns to the ballroom and lets me out of the cage. "Continue your silence, New Recruit," is all she says before she leads me to a plain black sedan that is parked out front. She is no longer wearing the collar or leash. Before I get in, she gives me my loincloth to put on when I arrive. We ride in the simple Mazda back to Mile High Stadium in Denver.

When I arrive, I see dozens of sweaty men on the field practicing the formations we learned yesterday. The group has developed quite a bit of precision and accuracy in their moves by this point. I am legitimately impressed by their talent, even as I wonder how I might be able to catch up.

"Go to your yard line and be a good boy," sissy Charlene says.

"Yes, sissy Charlene," I say as I get out of the car and head to the field. I am extremely hungry and feel embarrassed, but I try to suck it up and put on a brave face. I did not have time to take a shower, and I reek of body odor, cum, and booze. Plus, my stomach is growling. I hope we will get a break so that I can shower and eat soon. Somehow, despite my miserable morning, a rush of adrenaline propels me to participate with the other men in formation.

I run to my yard line and try to paint a smile on my face to hide my displeasure after spending the morning in the dog cage. The metal bars pressed so hard into my legs that I have indentations. I notice Quinn is throwing some quizzical glances my way.

I still have no clue what unfolded the night before, but I know I am making a very bad first impression on the three Mistresses. I pledge to myself I will do my best so I won't get kicked out. If I work hard and overcome my limitations, I can become an ideal submissive. I just know it!

The sun is growing high in the clear sky, and the temperature is quite warm. Several men are dripping sweat as they move up and down the field in tight block formations. I jog up to the open spot and fill the hole that was left for me. I can see two lines with 11 men each in front of me. I am right in the middle of another line with 5 men on either side of me, and there are six lines behind me. I estimate there are 99 men left here. A handful have definitely been ejected while I was stuck in the dog cage.

Butts, cocks, and balls jiggle underneath the loincloths all around me as the squadron of New Recruits march forward. Some men have tight, muscular rear ends, and others have flat or floppy behinds. I notice a few well-hung men, but most of the New Recruits seem to be pretty average in penis size. At least one man has an extremely small shaft that seems to be the size of my pinky finger. *The size of your devotional heart is what we care about,* a thought echoes in my mind, *and not your disgusting man meat!*

When I look up startled, I see Mistress Insomnia is staring at me from the stage. I remember to be on my best behavior. As we move, the Mistresses blow into metal whistles rhythmically, and the legions of men continuously salute on command with each sound of the whistle. I am physically exhausted and famished, but I ride my adrenaline rush for all I can to get through the next few hours.

In those hours, the Mistresses lead us through a spiral formation, teach us how to march in high step with pointed toes, and make us form multiple intersecting phalanxes that advance in a highly technical formation. The Mistresses mainly observe us from the tiered stage and shout commands through their bejeweled megaphones or whistle to direct us.

Occasionally, Mistress Doom cracks her bullwhip and makes a loud noise on the stage that startles men and makes them fall out of ranks. I stumble a few times, but other men tumble to the ground, and one even passes out on the sidelines from physical exertion. The Mistresses don't even bother to punish him; they merely have the sissy maids heave him over their shoulders and leave him outside the stadium gates. The man stays unconscious through it all. He appears a bit older and doesn't not seem to be very fit. I don't mind our ranks growing thinner at all.

The event organizers are sadistic, but they aren't completely heartless. Although they unceremoniously eject the man for his failure to serve, sissy maid Charlene does the man the dignity of calling a medic to make sure he is healthy before unlocking the man's chastity device and sliding a note into the waist of the man's loincloth. The note says, "Your luggage will be delivered to a locker at the Denver Airport. Call 1-800-MIS-TRES for more information. You are officially REJECTED from the Femdom Boot Camp, you miserable slug!"

By the evening, my throat is sore from shouting, "Yes, Mistress!" My arm is worn out from saluting, but I whip my hand up at each whistle without delay. My jiggly belly and pasty thighs have turned hot pink due to the sun shining down on the stadium all day. I hadn't even considered bringing sunscreen on this trip and wonder if I will get a chance to purchase any. I have a feeling that would be difficult, seeing as how I have not made the best first impression on the

Mistresses.

I wonder why the three gorgeous women are keeping me around. I hope and imagine it will be an erotic delight to serve them. I dream of kissing Mistress Doom's leather boots and massaging her beautiful ebony feet. I feel my cock grow hard again and begin to tug on the chastity contraption. sissy Charlene had locked me back in before I entered the field, but this time, I had been far from aroused. I feel pretty deflated by the bad first impression I've made here at Femdom Boot Camp.

This thing is definitely not going to fall off, I think. *I wonder what the heck happened when I wasn't here...?*

My train of thought is interrupted when the Mistresses dismount the stage and begin walking among us New Recruits. Mistress Insomnia slides past me in her tight leather catsuit and stiletto boots and gives me a tiny spanking with her leather gloved hand on my exposed butt cheek as she walks by. I leap in the air a little with surprise—and my dick leaps up as well with delight.

Just at that moment, I see young Oliver's head swivel. Mistress Insomnia is marching past the New Recruits and looking each one up and down. Mistress Doom and Mistress Intrigue follow her, with each Mistress brandishing her own unique flogging device. Mistress Doom has exchanged her wooden paddle for a lovely black leather flogger with long tails and a sturdy grip, and Mistress Intrigue has replaced her leather flogger with a cat-of-nine-tails.

Mistress Intrigue occasionally flicks her cat-of-nine-tails across a New Recruit's revealed derriere as she walks by in her leather hot pants and bikini. I can't help but wonder if it is a sign of displeasure…or affection. I know the little love-pat on my booty feels like positive attention to me and really turns me on. Mistress Intrigue has beautiful, long toned legs and a lovely figure.

I want to submit to all three of the Mistresses, but of all the Mistresses, I am the most drawn to Mistress Insomnia. Her image has been coming to me in dreams and visions even before I knew who she is! I can't help but wonder if we have some sort of psychic connection happening.

I practiced meditation as part of a philosophy class in college, and still do some Zen practice occasionally with a local group. It brings more meaning into my life than the stolid, rules-bound Catholic Church ever has, but I am not nearly as devoted and disciplined with my meditation practice as I could be.

That's not the only area where you lack discipline, I hear a woman snickering in my thoughts. I look up to see Mistress Insomnia smack her leather-gloved hand with the riding crop as she walks by me in her leather boots with precise steps. I wonder how she is able to walk so fluidly on such tiny stilettos on an uneven surface like the turf.

The Astroturf has been bothering my bare feet since

we've been practicing so many involved formations. I feel blisters forming. My right heel is tender, and my left ankle is swelling a bit. Plus, I feel exhausted and queasy from the remnants of alcohol swishing around in my system. I must be running off fumes at this point! Even though I am exceedingly weak, Mistress Insomnia's lithe leather-clad figure quickly catches and captivates my attention. I notice a sparkle near the ground as she walks past the line of men. Her boots have mirrors on the tops! *What the heck…?*

"You are now all fresh meat," Mistress Insomnia states through the diamond-studded megaphone. "You may be something special in your ordinary lives, but at Femdom Boot Camp, you are only here as long as the powerful Mistresses are pleased by you and your service. As you saw earlier today, we will not hesitate to punish you or eject you at will. "

Almost on cue, my stomach growls loudly. I hear someone snicker behind me. *Whoever it is probably feels he is better than me,* I imagine. *I have to prove him wrong and shape up!* Even though the punishment of being trapped in a dog cage for hours has been quite embarrassing and uncomfortable, all that time spent thinking in solitude has merely strengthened my resolve to achieve full submission and impress these Mistresses. If the militant suffragettes demanding the right to vote for women in the early 1900s could hunger fast and endure prison time, I can certainly go a morning without food to serve these goddesses.

"Or, you could eat," Mistress Insomnia says, and winks at me as she opens up a pull-tab can. Yet again, it seems she can read my thoughts. *Is anything private anymore?* I wonder. The tall Mistress dumps the contents into a metal dog food bowl and places the silver bowl on the Astroturf in front of me. I catch a vague whiff of something meaty. I glance down into the bowl and see what looks like beef covered in some type of gravy. It is quite clearly dog food.

"Don't worry. It's organic. In fact, it's better than what most people eat in the standard American diet," Mistress Insomnia explains. "I treat my pups well. Now eat," she commands, then grabs me by the hair on the back of my head and slowly pushes my head down into the bowl.

"Y-y-yes, Mistress," I stutter in the moment available before Mistress Insomnia plunges my face into the dog food bowl. I am extremely hungry, but even still the dish does not look very appealing by my typical standards. Living in New York City near so many gourmet restaurants and talented chefs has made me a bit of a foodie, and this is a far cry from my normal meal.

Still, I want to impress Mistress Insomnia and make up for the previous night's mistake. I have a brief moment wondering how Quinn and the other men will see me after this, and then, I submit completely and wholeheartedly. There is no turning back now.

In fact, I act as if I enjoy the food. I lap up every drop and then look up at Mistress Insomnia with what I imagined were cute puppy dog eyes (she thinks they appear hungover, dull, and stubborn, however).

As soon as I finish eating, I lose her attention. Mistress Insomnia motions for sissy Charlene to clear the bowl and food, then grabs her sparkling megaphone. "Now, stand still and at attention while I survey your ranks," Mistress Insomnia directs, and blows the whistle sharply. The men respond instantly, shouting, "Yes, Mistress" in unison, and then moving into formation.

I am starting to pick up on the rhythms and expectations around here at Femdom Boot Camp. While I missed learning many of the morning formations, I am getting good at the responses and salutes. I feel it might be possible to come back from the errors of last night.

I zone out for a moment. The golden whistle looks so beautiful against Mistress Insomnia's painted red mouth. She holds the whistle gracefully with her fingers, which are nestled into black leather gloves. Sadly, I feel much better after my pet food breakfast. The meaty dish absorbed a lot of the alcohol aftereffects and gave me more energy and strength.

I come out of my reverie when Mistress Insomnia blows the whistle again, then announces, "Move into second formation."

"Yes, Mistress!" I can hear Oliver shout, and all the men hold our hands to the brow in a military-style salute. I wrack my brain to figure out what the heck formation two is…

In the meantime, Mistress Insomnia approaches Oliver, who doesn't look a day over 18. The tall guy is clearly nervous and keeps awkwardly clearing his throat. But even though he looks and seems young, I know he certainly is over 18 since our IDs had been strictly vetted during the background check.

"Now that's a good boy," Mistress Insomnia coos, as she runs her leather-clad finger across his cheek. Oliver melts. He loves the feel of leather on his skin. She grabs the boy's jaw and lifts his chin as if to kiss him. He holds his breath, suspended in disbelief as the powerful Mistress brings her lips centimeters away from his own and stares into his eyes for what feels like forever.

Before Oliver knows what to think, Mistress Insomnia has taken a step back and points her booted foot out. She is looking down at the mirror, which, much to Oliver's embarrassment, is reflecting back his package for her viewing pleasure. The skinny boy's cheeks are flushing pink with humiliation. "This one can stay," Mistress Insomnia states matter-of-factly and taps his chastity cage.

As Mistress Intrigue passes, she commands Oliver, "About face!" He turns around and exposes his bare butt by pulling the loincloth flap up. "Assume the position!" Oliver bends forward slightly and puts his hands on knees, sticking his booty out. All color has drained from his already pale face, and his eyes are downcast.

"My, my, you are a good boy, aren't you?" Mistress Doom says, and she pulls the leather tassels of her flogger over his bare skin to tease him. At this point, I have to admit I am getting a bit jealous. I came here to submit to these Mistresses and they haven't paid me any attention, other than the close call with Quinn when we arrived and with the whole dog cage punishment situation...

I know submissives are to be seen and not heard, so I am not sure how to catch their eye. It feels petty, but I am even jealous of Oliver's youth. *Why is this young guy getting all the attention? Do I even have a chance?* My thoughts keep racing, bringing up all of my inner insecurities. I feel a jumble of anxious tension fill my body and slosh around, mixing with the dog food that is now digesting.

I hate to admit it, and I don't tell many folks, but I have a lot of self-doubt. I try to keep a brave face and seem strong as a hedge fund manager, but I've seen enough counselors to know I am plagued by insecurities because of a huge abandonment wound from childhood.

Something about my birth mother giving me up for adoption makes me feel like I did something wrong, to make her leave me. I know it's not logical, but a child part of myself hates myself, and fears that something about me is unlovable, because the woman who gave birth to me did not want to raise me. So, in my emotional brain, if my mother couldn't love me, who can?

Even though my incredibly wealthy adoptive parents invited me into their family of three kids and a nanny, and they cared well for me—I always had plenty of food, lived in a nice house in the Upper East Side, and attended a prestigious school where I excelled—I have never felt complete.

And no, in case you're wondering, I've never met my birth mother. All I know is that she was pretty young when she gave me up, based on some files from the adoption agency, and that she lived near Queens in New York. Maybe one day I'll discover more about my roots. I have thought maybe I've seen her in visions and dreams, and often I wonder if she might be in a nearby crowd. I wonder what her life was like, and who my father had been…

My thoughts are interrupted by the slap of the flogger across Oliver's pale ass. The young man jumps slightly at the first impact, and his butt cheek becomes slightly pink. Mistress Doom places her leather-gloved hand and presses down on his hips.

"What do you say, boy?" she asks.

"Th-th-thank you, Mistress," Oliver stutters.

"That's right. You've been such a good boy today that you will get a treat. Mistress Insomnia?"

Mistress Intrigue approaches Oliver and winks at Mistress Doom. Mistress Intrigue moves her bikini triangle to the side, and Mistress Doom reaches down and lowers a flap sewn into her leather catsuit. My jaw drops open when I realize they each had exposed one of their breasts.

Mistress Doom has beautiful nipples, and—not to be crass—I suddenly understand why some breasts are called melons. Her breasts are that large, and equally juicy. I notice my mouth watering as I look at her large dark brown nipple against her darker brown skin. I try not to get caught staring, but I feel like my eyes are magnetically drawn to her bosom.

Mistress Intrigue has pert and perky breasts, the kind that would fit perfectly into your hand. Her tiny nipple is hard, like it is a New Recruit standing at attention. The women's exposed breasts are even more striking against the black leather outfits that they wear.

"Time for your treat, Oliver," Mistress Intrigue says. "Come here and suck our nipples like a good boy. Be sure to moan and let everyone know how lovely they are."

"Yes, M-m-Mistresses!" Oliver says nervously. His cock strains against the cage, and he is acutely aware of the almost 100 men and the three mistresses watching him. He wraps his lips around Mistress Intrigue's nipple and sucks gently, moaning loudly so all can hear him.

"Good boy. Now service Mistress Doom."

"Yes, Mistress," Oliver says. He begins suckling Mistress Doom's beautiful melon. So badly he wishes he could squeeze it. "Mistress Doom?" he asks. "Can I p-p-please squeeze your beautiful breast?"

I gasp. I can't believe that newbie got up the guts to ask for a special reward. Would she let him? I certainly want to squeeze one of those boobies myself.

"You can do that, but only if you'll also lick my pussy here in front of everyone and make me cum," Mistress Doom says.

Oliver blushes. He has actually never fooled around to that extent with his high school girlfriend. He is willing to try, but what if he messes it up? Plus, what about everyone watching?

Mistress Intrigue notices his embarrassment.

"You!" she says to me, and flicks the cat-of-nine-tails across my upper arm. "Can't you see he is nervous? You're older, wiser, more experienced. Are you willing to show him how it's done on me?"

"Uh, yes," I mutter, caught entirely off guard. Yet again, my day has taken an unexpected turn.

"Yes what?" Mistress Intrigue asks, as she slaps my bare ass with the cat-of-nine-tails. She hits me so hard, I feel momentarily dazed, and I don't answer. Before I know what happened, the tall, thin Mistress grabs my hands and pulls me up on stage. She expertly and coldly locks my hands into a pillory, then commands me to bend over and lift my ass high up in the air. Mistress Intrigue spanks me bare butt again, and I jump slightly at the impact.

"Oh, uh, yes, Mistress! No disrespect meant. I'm just learning," I stammer.

Mistress Intrigue slaps my ass with the cat-of-nine-tails again, this time quite hard. She uses her wrist to add an extra painful snap at the end, and I leap up at the impact. I feel a slight sting where each knot on the implement hits me. I glance at Mistress Intrigue's beautiful angelic face and notice her grin grow larger the more uncomfortable I become. She is clearly quite sadistic, and, somewhat to my surprise, I find her sadism turns me on. I wonder, *Am I subconsciously trying to get punished?*

"Now, dog!" Mistress Intrigue snarls, as she grabs my ear and pulls me to attention. "Listen up and stop acting like such a little bitch. I've heard all about your disobedience, and it is already testing my patience. Here at Femdom Boot Camp we expect our submissives to be of the finest caliber, with impeccable grooming and gentlemanly manners. Do you understand, New Recruits?"

"Yes, Mistress," the men respond in unison—except for one. I hear someone in the back join in a few seconds too late. The timid voice chimes in with "Oh—yes, Mistress!" Mistress Insomnia marches across the Astroturf in her thigh-high glossy black leather boots and administers a powerful spanking to the late man using her leather gloved hand. I hear a loud, "OUCH!!!!" The man's white skin is marked with red marks from the impact, and he tries to stifle his cries of pain.

Mistress Insomnia looks lovely in her skintight leather catsuit that shows off her figure. Her luxurious suit includes a carefully boned corset that greatly enhances her beautiful bustline. Mistress Intrigue looks smoking hot, but she is pissed at the man, whom I learned later was named Earl Chapman.

"What's that?" I hear Mistress Intrigue ask insistently, as she grabs Earl's ear. I glance at the man more intently. He appears to be in his early twenties, and I am glad someone else is finally making a mistake besides me. Honestly, the dude is so buff, I am pleased he is getting some negative attention. Maybe this will take him down a notch and give me an advantage. In that moment, I vow to work out and lift some weights to try to reduce my beer belly and to be sexy for the Mistresses if they keep me around.

"I'm sorry, but I'm really not sure, Mistress," Earl stammers with a country twang that sounds similar to Mistress Doom's. "Please help me be a good boy. I am so sorry."

"Except for 'Yes, Mistress' and 'More, Mistress,' submissives are to be seen and not heard," Mistress Insomnia shouts through the megaphone to the group. Bored of disciplining Earl, she moves about 5 yard lines away from him and continues to use her mirror boots to inspect the New Recruit's packages while Mistresses Doom and Intrigue, Oliver, and I are up on stage.

I look around and notice every man on the field is still watching what is unfolding with me and Oliver up on stage. It is slightly comical to look up and see an army of loincloth-clad men stationed on yard lines across the field at Mile High Stadium. And now they are all about to watch me orally pleasure these powerful dominatrixes. I can't believe this is actually happening…

I never told anyone, but I am actually into exhibitionism. I love the idea of other people watching me have sex and getting off on it. My college girlfriend had always complimented my oral technique, so I felt I was up to this challenge.

"Yes, Mistress," Earl shouts from the field.

"Good boy," Mistress Insomnia continues to pace the ranks and inspect the men. She pauses in a few spots to angle the mirror just right so she can check out each New Recruit's full package.

In the meantime, Mistress Intrigue reaches for a key on a large keyring she has hanging from a leather belt around her waist. She inserts the key into my pillory and opens the top. She fits me with a narrow leather collar, then attaches a chain leash to it and leads me to a part of the stage that features beautiful thrones. I really feel like a dog now.

Mistress Doom does the same with Oliver. On the stage are two velvet thrones, with gilded edges. Mistress Doom unzips a zipper that runs from jer belly to her back, and Mistress Intrigue removes her leather hot pants, exposing their crotches to Oliver and I, the submissives. The powerful Mistresses sit down and spread their booted legs.

"Submissives, on your knees."

"Yes, Mistress," we both intone. I think of Mistress Intrigue bending over and imagine me fucking her from behind. Her slim hips are really sexy. I feel my cock get hard and push a bit against the cock ring, which is definitely plenty tight…

"No need to look me in the eye, slave," Mistress Intrigue snarls. "Submissives must never look any of us in our eyes unless commanded to do so."

"Yes, Mistress," I reply with confidence. This is my opportunity to really win her favor and overcome the challenges from my rough arrival.

"And remember, this is because women are superior to men in every possible way, and you slave-submissives are the lowest on the totem pole," Mistress Doom adds.

"Yes, Mistress," the group shouts in unison. I marvel that after only one day of training the large group of New Recruits is doing so well.

"Get started, worms" Mistress Intrigue calls from her throne.

I am ready. Now that I have some food—albeit dog food—in my belly, I have some energy, and I am going to let myself shine! I lower my eyes and sink my head between Mistress Intrigue's legs. I smell her distinct womanly aroma and notice I am getting even more aroused. I instinctually go to rub my cock, but I feel the sharp sting of a leather whip on my hand as I touch myself.

"No, no, no!" Mistress Intrigue cries, as she whips my exposed hand several more times, even drawing a bit of blood. "This is not about you. It's about me! Your sole purpose for existing is to bring me pleasure. Do you understand, slave?"

"Yes, Mistress." I begin licking her clit and lapping up the juices that have started flowing out of her pussy. I notice she relaxes and seems to be enjoying herself, so I use my hands to massage her breasts and belly gently. Her head falls backwards and her eyes roll back into her head. She keeps pressing up against my mouth and moaning.

"Keep going, boy," she says. "Good job."

To me, both the Mistress's scent and taste are heavenly. I enjoy feeling her squirm as I move my tongue around her nether regions. I look up and see that she has exposed both of her breasts and is fondling her nipples. It really turns me on that she is so turned on. I want to fuck her so badly, and I would not mind taking her right there in front of everyone.

Out of nowhere, I remember an interesting orgy experience that I had while I was in college. I have always wanted to have another one but never found the right opportunity. I notice my mind spiraling off into a group sex fantasy as I go down on Mistress Intrigue.

As I continue to lick and suck her pussy, I can't help but imagine the other two Mistresses suddenly joining in. Mistress Doom would spank me and call me her slave. She would make me kiss her shiny boots and beg on my knees before I could fuck her—in front of everyone, while no one else got to have her.

And of course, I would only get the chance after Mistress Intrigue was quite satisfied. In my fantasy,

Mistress Intrigue would come out and say, "Let me try him." Then she would blindfold me and sit on my face while I squirmed. Mistress Doom would continue to ride my cock, and the two women would fondle each other. I thought that would be such sweet pleasure.

Eventually, Mistress Intrigue would come, and Mistress Insomnia would ride me. I imagined hearing them all admiring my cock and my stamina. All the other New Recruits would be so jealous of me! That would be amazing. And I mean, you never know. The other orgy had happened just as unexpectedly...

In college, I'd ended up at our favorite dive bar after another amazing basketball game. All of the NYU students were celebrating by taking copious shots. Pretty soon these turned into body shots, and I remembered hoisting a cute young co-ed onto the bar. She was wearing a short plaid pleated skirt and had her college T-shirt tied in a knot at her waist so her flat belly was exposed.

I couldn't help but glance at her white panties under her skirt as I lifted her up to the bar, and she twirled and lay down. She even had white knee socks that went all the way up her calves, and she was wearing cute short black lace-up boots. This particular girl was definitely known as a party girl who liked to have a lot of fun, and I knew she'd already hooked up with at least two of my fraternity brothers. Both of them happened to be right there, also getting drunk and celebrating the victory.

The girl—Matilda was her name—laid down on the bar with her knees up and her legs spread. She pulled her shirt up even higher, and the bartender poured some tequila into her belly button. I could see the smooth bottoms of her breasts emerging from under her shirt, and her nipples stood erect and hard. There were dozens of drunk people celebrating in the bar who were cheering and hollering. Matilda was super-hot.

I placed a lime wedge and some salt on her smooth belly for a belly shot. My fraternity brothers (including Quinn) started chanting, "Do it! Do it! Do it!" I was totally hard by this point. I sucked the tequila out of Matilda's exposed belly button, took the lime wedge in my mouth and squeezed the juice out, then licked the salt.

I immediately wished I was licking some other part of her, and I started to kiss her belly down towards her skirt. She giggled with a drunken laugh. I expected her to push my head away, but she actually angled her lower body toward my mouth and pushed my head further down. Everyone at the bar laughed and cheered.

So, I kept going. I kissed her over the short skirt and then buried my head underneath the skirt, kissing her through the white panties. She giggled like it tickled and shouted, "Feels so good!" And she opened her legs wider and pressed against my face, with her hips buckling against the bar.

The bartender lined up another slice of lime, a bit of salt, and tequila in Matilda's belly. While I continued to pleasure her beneath her skirt, my fraternity brother Kyle took the shot from her belly button, sucked the lime, and licked the salt. She started massaging his hard cock through his pants while the crowd continued to cheer. At this point I was way more into this than celebrating the basketball win.

Kyle motioned to Eric, the other fraternity brother that the girl had previously fucked, and the bartender prepared another shot. Meanwhile, Matilda was going wild with desire. I was now gently fingering her through her panties, and I could feel a wet spot forming underneath my touch. She was bucking her hips and moaning, but trying not to move so much that she ruined her orgasm. She was clearly getting off on everyone watching her. *Was this the sexual liberation I'd been learning about in my women's studies electives?* My intellectual mind would not shut up! I brought my attention back to the physical sensations of pleasuring Matilda.

Her right hand was stroking Kyle's long member through his pants. I couldn't help but notice that Kyle seemed quite blessed in that department. Kyle was moaning, and his eyes were rolling back into his head.

He grabbed Eric's hand and pulled him toward Matilda. Eric went face first into her belly button and sucked up the tequila before he sucked the lime and licked up the salt. Matilda giggled and said, "I want more, boys!"

With another drunken laugh, Matilda pulled her shirt up over her breasts. They were nice and full, probably a C cup, and they sat nicely on her body. Eric went right over and started suckling on her tit, while she continued to stroke Eric's now-hard cock. I began to rub her belly as I continued to nuzzle through her panties against her vagina.

"More!" she shouted drunkenly. She was clearly enjoying herself. I looked up at the bartender. I was kind of worried we were going to get in trouble or something, but I noticed actually that the bartender had started stroking his own cock through his pants, and when I looked around there were dozens of people in the bar cheering and watching. Nobody seemed bothered whatsoever, least of all Matilda.

"I want to feel you all inside of me," she said, winking at Kyle. "I already know how wonderful that is with a few of you, so let's start with the new one, Cleo."

"My name's Theo—Theodore," I murmured.

"Oh yeah, sure. Whatever, Theodore," she said. "Just get that a hard cock inside my wet pussy!"

At this point, I definitely wanted to pound her pussy hard. I'd been drinking pretty heavily, and by now, all of my inhibitions were gone. Thankfully I wasn't in a small town, so it's not like I would run into someone I knew besides my frat brothers... New York was a huge, anonymous city, and my fraternity brothers were clearly already into this sort of thing. We were always bragging and sharing stories of our conquests. So, why not move forward here together?

I started by slowly pulling off Matilda's panties, teasing her as I exposed her clitoris and vagina to the patrons at the bar. The bartender continued to stroke his cock, and I noticed a few couples seemed to be discreetly pleasuring each other under the table in their shared booths.

Meanwhile, Matilda was still pleasuring Kyle, and Eric continued to suckle on her breasts. The two men were moaning in ecstasy. Everyone in the bar had stopped what they were doing and were just watching. I noticed quite a few people had their hands under the bar, and I figured they might be pleasuring themselves as they watched. Feeling the support of the crowd, I pulled the panties all the way down Matilda's long legs and whirled them over my head like a lasso. The men and women in the bar cheered rowdily.

The bar was a little elevated, but it was low enough to the ground that I was able to swing Matilda's hips towards me and lower them just enough so that I could penetrate her easily. I used the pre-cum from my cock as lubrication and then plunged my penis into her very wet pussy. As I began to pump in and out, she started moaning and shouting "Yes! Yes!"

Her pussy was really tight, and it squeezed my cock hard. All the people in the bar could watch my bare ass thrusting against her because my shorts had fallen to the ground. I kept pounding her for ten or fifteen minutes until Kyle was ready for his turn.

"Let me in, man," Kyle said. I glanced over and saw the pink swollen head of his cock was ready for the task at hand.

So, I pulled out—later I was especially glad. In my drunken stupor I hadn't thought to use any protection, and the last thing I needed was an unplanned pregnancy with a party girl that I barely knew. Thankfully the STD test I took later came out clean as well. The combination of liquor and sex had overridden my better judgment, so I was glad that everything turned out OK.

When I pulled out, my dick was still swollen and dark pink. It was covered in Matilda's juices.

"Come here," she said, and gestured toward her face.

I went to her face, and she turned her mouth to the side and took my whole cock down her throat. I started to fuck her face, and she moaned and writhed just as Kyle shoved his sizable member into her pussy.

Eric took a break from suckling her breasts and started to fondle them instead, moving them in gentle circles on her chest, and pinching the nipples between his fingers. Her moans were slightly muffled since my 6-inch cock was filling her mouth. Kyle had a look of great pleasure on his face as he pumped in and out. A young brunette woman at the bar slapped Kyle's exposed ass and accidentally spilled her beer.

Things were getting really rowdy. I came in Matilda's mouth, and backed away and sat down so I could soak up the pleasure. As I pulled up my shorts again, I looked around and noticed that even more people had their pants down by their ankles, with their hands mysteriously disappeared under their tables.

One redhead had her eyes rolled back into the back of her head, and she was cupping her breast and jiggling it as she watched. Another gorgeous blonde woman had pulled both her breasts out of her tight cocktail dress and was massaging her nipples as she observed the orgy. A sleek Latina woman in a tight mini skirt winked at me from the other side of the bar. This place was a dive, but the chicks were gorgeous!

The bartender had stopped serving and was just watching from the front row view. After a while, Kyle came inside of Matilda, and her whole body shuddered with delight.

"Now it's my turn," Eric said. "Saving the best for last, huh, Matilda?"

“Mmmm,” was all Matilda could manage to say, in her state of erotic arousal.

Eric pulled her down off the bar, turned her around, and pushed her forward so that he could penetrate her doggy style. He pulled her plaid skirt up so that her full butt was exposed, with her long legs clad in knee socks reaching down to the ground. As he fucked her, he spanked her hard.

Eric had smooth, dark skin that contrasted against Matilda's pale white skin. I noticed I was almost hypnotized watching Eric pound Matilda from behind. She was screaming and shrieking, "I'm going to come! I'm going to come!" Eric just kept going, thrusting hard, and then Matilda came. She let out a loud yelp, a moan, and then collapsed onto the bar, with her butt still stuck up in the air. She looked like she was ready for a nap.

Eric slowly pulled his long black cock out of her white shaved pussy, and I noticed a mix of their juices dripping out of her. They pooled onto the bar, where Kyle in his drunken stupor went and licked them all up, right before licking her pussy and shoving his tongue inside to taste everyone’s juices together.

Kyle and Eric winked at me. “Welcome to the fraternity, bro,” Kyle said. Kyle smacked me playfully on the butt.

“Can’t wait till the next game,” Eric said.

“Me either,” I added.

The crowd at the bar cheered and ordered another

round of drinks.

★

8: Stamina

All of a sudden, I am brought back to reality by the feeling of sharp fingernails being drawn sharply down my back. There is no orgy… My head is still between Mistress Intrigue's legs. After I feel her fingernails on my back, I glance up at her alluring eyes.

She lowers her gaze to me and admonishes me: "Submissives must never look the Mistresses directly in the eye. Do you understand, slave?"

"Yes, Mistress."

"Now, that's a good boy, Theodore," Mistress Intrigue murmurs. *She knows my name?!? Is that a good or bad sign?* My thoughts spiral out of control.

"You are released from duty," she tells me after what feels like hours of very public pussy licking.

I say a muffled, "Yes, Mistress," with my tongue still pressed inside her vagina. I lap up a few more of her juices before I raise my head.

"I have achieved a sufficient level of sexual satisfaction," she says. I feel a sharp tap on my shoulder, and Mistress Intrigue pushes my head back from between her legs. She uses her hand to motion that I should stand up, and I obey. She forcefully grabs my shoulders and turns me around, then spanks my bare ass before sending me back to the lineup of men. I feel both embarrassed and proud that the whole group of New Recruits has witnessed my skills. I pass by Quinn, and he winks at me. I feel my pathetic cock stir a bit and fill the chastity cage when I receive his attention.

What exactly happened last night? I think. *Did Quinn and I—no way!* I have never been with a man before, and so I definitely don't think one of my college fraternity brothers should be the first dude I explore my sexuality with. That just seems wrong for some reason. Although I have absolutely no issues with anyone having consensual sex with anyone else, I still feel stigmatized in my own behavior. Even though things seem free and open here at Femdom Boot Camp, I realize I am still abiding by the values and norms that have been indoctrinated in me since childhood.

So, perhaps my discomfort at the thought of hooking up with Quinn is because Quinn is from my past, and my past self, my naive self, was inhibited, was judgmental, was small in thought, and tended to conform to rules and standards. In some ways, it is easier to consider getting with sissy Charlene than with Quinn, just because sissy Charlene is so outside my normal life, and has only known me as a New Recruit, and nothing more.

On top of my apparent physical attraction to Quinn, I want to kiss Mistress Intrigue so bad, and let her taste her juices on my lips, but I dare not ask. Quinn tells me later that I gave the Mistress oral pleasure on stage for about 45 minutes, not three hours. In the meantime, Mistress Insomnia ejected a few more men based on the mirror boot test while the oral examination was taking place on stage. The rest of the dozens of remaining New Recruits all stood in place watching the whole time.

Mistress Insomnia orders the men to stand absolutely still, and then uses a powerful bullwhip to zap anyone who moves, twitches, or even blinks during that time. Quinn says he has heard at least 100 to 200 lashings falling on various men during my time on stage. Only one man says, "Ouch," and Mistress Insomnia promptly removes him.

"Your pain inconveniences us," she shouts through her megaphone at the vocal man. "Since submissives are to be seen and not heard, I'm afraid we can't handle you here. Leave now. Please follow sissy Charlene to pack your bags. Charlene will arrange your ride to the airport.

The man is so stunned, he doesn't even say, "Yes, Mistress." Everyone else is catching on well, though. When Mistress Insomnia says, "It's only fair that the unruly are removed," the remaining New Recruits saluted proudly and call out, "Yes, Mistress."

"That's more like it, boys!" Mistress Insomnia

shouts with glee.

Seeing such obedience among the rank-and-file New Recruits, I notice that my cock is definitely pulsing with pleasure inside its cage. I feel a sweet pleasure knowing I no longer own my own cock, and that I am now giving all of my pleasure to the Mistresses and existing to serve them. I feel a sort of transcendent bliss as the energy of selfless service begins flowing in and through me. I can't really explain what I am accessing, but I think it's what is called the sub state. It is what drew me to *Kinky Times* to begin with.

After seeing *50 Shades of Grey*, I got a glimpse into a form of sexuality that was more that the cookie-cutter normative bullshit I'd been taught, but I related more to the submissive role than the dominant one. I want to deepen my submission and find true meaning in life. For me, the path to complete submission is more than sexual. It is spiritual. It is a deeper yearning, a strong passion, that comes from within. And now that the seeds of desire have been watered in me, I feel something come alive deep inside. I am super intrigued to gain more self-knowledge and insight through my path to complete submission at Femdom Boot Camp.

As I muse through my thoughts and return to my

place in line, the younger man on stage also tries to raise his head. Mistress Doom orders Oliver, "That does not apply to you! Keep going." She is sitting on the raised throne, which is lined with red velvet. Her long legs are spread wide, and her dark pussy is exposed by the fully unzipped crotch of her leather catsuit. Oliver, a slightly awkward and lanky boy, is kneeling uncomfortably on his knees with his head pressed into her nether regions. Her tall, lace-up boots frame his body.

Oliver has been trying hard to tease her clit with light strokes of his tongue, but she keeps pushing harder into his face and telling him to go deeper inside her. When he pushes his tongue into her canal, she moans and softens a little, but she gets upset when he stops after 30 minutes or so.

"I am still unsatisfied, and you are not released from duty," Mistress Doom tells the 18-year-old. "You might need to learn to use your fingers, too. Have you ever fingered a woman, boy?"

"No, Mistress. My only girlfriend wouldn't even let me French kiss her."

"Well, I hate to be rude, but that explains A LOT," Mistress Doom replies.

"Boy! Go help him," Mistress Intrigue directs me.

"Yes, Mistress," I say, and shuffle over next to Oliver on the elevated stage. The younger man's loincloth covers his ass crack, but I can see his skinny cock clad in a cock cage poking out the front. Oliver is paying no attention to his appearance. He seems wholeheartedly devoted to pleasing his demanding Mistress. I stand next to the young man in his leather loincloth, wishing I had tried to diet a bit before coming all the way out here. My sizeable gut is hanging down over my loincloth, and it stands out more in contrast with Oliver's skinny physique.

"Just put your fingers like this, and then make a slight curling motion," I demonstrate with two fingers. "And don't put them in until her vagina naturally invites them. It's up to you to make her so turned on that she's lubricated and ready for you. You can always add more fingers once she's warmed up."

Oliver glances up at Mistress Doom, his head still buried in her cooch. "Yes, boy, listen to him," she says. Oliver starts with just his pinky finger before Mistress Doom tells him to add more fingers. "Make them nice and thick, unlike that package of yours," she jokes. "I've never seen such a skinny excuse for a cock!"

"Yes, Mistress!" Oliver begins pumping her pussy with three, then four, fingers twisted together. She starts moaning and pushing her hips toward him. He curls his finger the way I had shown him, and her pussy juices begin streaming down his fingers. Oliver uses his tongue to lap up all of the juices. From my vantage point, it seems the young man is actually enjoying himself. I have to admit, though, that I am glad at least that my experience gives me a leg up on the dude. I definitely can't compete as far as body shape or youthfulness...

"Good boy," Mistress Doom moans. "Keep it up."

Oliver continues to worship her pussy, and Mistress Intrigue comes over and hands Mistress Doom a miniature battery-operated vibrator. Mistress Doom runs it gently over her clit and starts bucking even harder on Oliver's fingers. He keeps up the pressure and within minutes feels her pussy throbbing and pulsing around them. A thick white cream coats his fingers. She collapses in ecstatic bliss and moans. "That is good. You may now stop," Mistress Doom states.

"Yes, Mistress. But can I please get one more taste of your pussy juices?"

"If you're a good boy and do what you're told, one day you just might. But for now, suckle the titty treat I promised you, then get back in line," she replies.

I can't believe the shy young man asked the bold questions that I am afraid to vocalize. Mistress Doom invites Oliver's mouth to suck her exposed nipple, then spanks the lad's pale ass and sends him back to his yard line.

Quinn observes the scene up on stage and checks in with himself. He feels a bit at an advantage. Quinn is physically fit, and the younger man is scrawny. Quinn used to be married, so he'd definitely learned how to pleasure a woman after having sex with the same partner hundreds of times.

Quinn tells me later, when I confess my insecurity about my weight, that Mistress Intrigue had not even noticed my big gut while I was going down on her. Quinn says he saw that she had her eyes rolled back in her head practically the entire time, and her legs had been shaking.

And Quinn is just one of the remaining group of almost 100 New Recruits. Each one has a unique reaction to the morning's events. sissy Charlene coaches us all to write our honest thoughts each night in our submissive diaries, so that the Mistresses would know how to train each one of us.

Kahua's Submissive Diary, Day 1

Dear Diary,

My powerful Mistress says I must write my thoughts in this journal each day. Today I saw lots of things. I felt aroused and wanted to touch myself, but I knew I couldn't, because my member now belongs to the Mistresses. And the pleasure of knowing I am theirs is beginning to drive me wild. I can see I am nothing special here, so only my true submission and obedience can make me stand out. I am honored for the opportunity and hope to please each Mistress.

Signed, Yard Line 32S (Kahua)

We had a long day at Mile High Stadium that day. Once the Mistresses are sexually satisfied, they begin to put the Arousal Army through the paces. First came some physical discipline and inspection. The remaining New Recruits are lined up in front of the stage, with the 10 with the best dicks in the front row. Mistress Insomnia has chosen her favorite during the mirror boot inspection that morning.

sissy Charlene, the servant maid, has instructed the men to stand with feet hips' width apart, arms hanging by their side, and chins up. Just like the British guard, they are not to move unless directed, and are to remain constantly at attention for any whim of the Mistresses.

First, Mistress Insomnia raises her bejeweled megaphone and shouts, "Boys, raise your arms in front of you to shoulder height. Keep them there." The men raise their arms and wait. The Mistresses begin pacing up and down in front of the line of loincloth clad men. As she walks by a short and stocky man, Mistress Insomnia hears a slight whimper. She turns to its source.

“Are you happy to serve your Mistress?” she asks him. Her ice blue eyes practically glow in the high afternoon sunlight.

He whimpers again, this time louder.

“Yes, Mistress,” says sissy Charlene, who is helping train the New Recruits by example.

“Oh, yes, Mistress!” Lane, the whimpering man says. “But… It does hurt to hold one’s arms up this long. Surely you don’t expect us to continue for much longer? I’m tired.”

“Submissives are to be seen and not heard!” Mistress Insomnia blares through her megaphone. "sissy Charlene, see this man out."

The sissy maid runs over on heels to Lane, places her manicured hand on Lane’s lower back, grabs his arm and gently guides him back to the locker room. "I'll be removing your chastity device before you leave. You are no longer allowed to participate, and you must go now.”

“What? Surely I get another chance!” Lane shouts. The men on the field can still hear him; he is so loud. “No! I paid good money to be here!”

“This is not the place for you, and I am going to have to ask you to leave now,” sissy Charlene says. “Trust me, buddy. If you thought that was bad, you’re not fit to serve these Mistresses. This is nothing.”

Back on the field, the remaining 70-odd men keep their arms held in front of them. My arms have started shaking with the effort. I glance at Quinn, whose muscular arms seem to be resting easily in the position. Quinn makes everything in life look easy...

Things are never that easy for me. I feel like I am about to pass out when a mental image of Mistress Insomnia fills my mind's eye. She is dressed head to toe in a skintight latex catsuit, and her skin seems extra pale in contrast with her bright red lipstick and black eyeliner.

"You can do it, boy," the mental image says, and the mirage of Mistress Insomnia blows me a kiss. "Don't give up. Be patient." The image slowly fades away, and I become aware of my surroundings: the stadium seats surrounding the cadre of 70-or-so bare-chested and bare-assed men, all with arms raised, trying to impress the Mistresses with their submission.

What the...? I think. I blink my eyes and realize the mental image has just been a fantasy. Still, I feel oddly rejuvenated and like I can keep my arms raised for even longer. But I am puzzled by the image. Mistress Insomnia isn't even wearing latex. She has on leather, and she is down near the shorter men at the end of the line. *What does that image mean?*

After 10 more minutes, seven men are definitely faltering. One freckled redhead, Thomas, keeps accidentally lowering his arms, then raising them back up. I recognize him from the group in my limousine when I arrived. Thomas is literally dripping sweat, and his face looks filled with nervousness and pain.

"Keep your arms raised, boy!" Mistress Doom says, as she gently paddles Thomas's bare white ass. Thomas is only 22 and comes from a very wealthy Boston family. He pretended he needed money to enhance his stock portfolio investments, and convinced his mother and father to bequeath $500,000 to him from his trust fund. They have no idea he used it instead to invest in his kinky future by coming to the audition for the Arousal Army.

"Yes, Mistress!" Thomas replies, jumping a bit at the impact of the paddle. "I'm—I'm trying!"

"Boy, don't try—do! Do!" Mistress Doom shouts. "Do you see, New Recruits, that women are clearly superior to men?"

"Yes, Mistress!" Thomas shouts, and it is clear he is still struggling. His arms are continuously dipping lower and lower, and his muscles are shaking. His pale face is contorted in pain, and he is tensing his jaw. The other men echo, "Yes, Mistress," and one high-pitched voice shouts, "Women are clearly superior."

I notice a bemused smile on Mistress Doom's lips when she hears the comment. Her eyes fall on Thomas again, and her lip curls up into a snarl.

"Boy, that is not satisfactory," Mistress Doom says. "You simply do not have what it takes. sissy

Charlene, remove him, and the others who are shaking."

"Yes, Mistress," the sissy maid exclaims with a chirpy enthusiasm from behind the line of men. "I see that yard lines 15S, 34N, 49S, 22N, 7N, 6N, and 40S are all shaking." Thomas is on yard line 6N.

"Everyone he just called, get out!" Mistress Doom thunders through her diamond-encrusted megaphone.

"Yes, Mistress," shouts the sissy maid. The men who were cut look around with dismay. Some are massaging their arms or shaking them out due to the stress. Some hang their heads and look despondent. Thomas is in a bit of shock. Are they talking about him?

"That means you, boy," Mistress Doom says, and gives Thomas another paddling. "Back to the locker room, all of you, to remove your cock cages and return your loincloths. Never come back!"

At that, she and the other three Mistresses start guffawing and laughing, as if it were a joke. I don't think it is funny, but of course, I keep my thoughts to myself. I've done enough to stand out already, and at this point, I just want to blend in and coast a bit.

That's what you think, Mistress Insomnia's voice rose up in his mind. *You think no one knows what you think. But I know.*

I look up and see Mistress Insomnia staring at me from the stage. She winks and smiles once she catches my eye. I look around as if to see if she meant to wink at someone else. But I am the only one there. *What does this all mean…?* For now, I have no idea. Maybe I am just exhausted from the physical exertion I've been through, and my mind is playing tricks on me. Maybe there was something weird in the dog food I had for lunch. Either way, I was proud I survived. I am not ready to go home yet.

I imagine that young Thomas feels ashamed that he had essentially wasted his parent's money on what turned out to be a quick rejection. In the locker room, I had heard a few of the men grumbling about surrendering the cash they'd paid to be there.

"Bunch of bitches, they weren't even hot. I'd never fuck a single one of them," an overweight older man mutters under his breath.

"Don't you realize I can hear you?" sissy Charlene asks, and dangles the key in front of the man's face. "I am extremely loyal to my Mistresses and will not tolerate you demeaning them. You get time out. Go sit in that corner for 20 minutes, and then, if you behave, I will remove your cock from its well-deserved cage."

"No."

"You don't get to say. Wait there."

The man looks around, baffled. The other rejected men who have been sent to the locker room stare silently at the disobedient man. It is clear nobody is going to come to his assistance. He briefly considers running, but realizes he would still have the chastity device on. The man can't handle the thought of going to a sex store and asking for help with a removal. *Would that even work, or would he have to go to the hospital? Would this thing ever come off without the key?*

It is too much to consider, so he gives up and sits in the corner for 20 minutes and stays silent, even though he is seething inside. While the disobedient man is in punishment, sissy Charlene removes the cock cages from the seven other rejected men, including Thomas, and sends them on their way. The Mistresses are now down to 75 potential New Recruits.

Mistress Insomnia makes one more pass in front of the line of men. This time, she focuses on their fingernails.

"You!" she shouts at one of the men, who is still standing with his arms outstretched.

"Yes, Mistress?" he says, with a tinge of nervousness to his voice.

"You're out. Get a manicure, buddy."

"What do you mean?" He looks down at his hands, puzzled.

"Are you a gardener or something? You could grow plants with the amount of dirt under your fingernails. We expect our stable of submissives to be a bit more polished than that. sissy Charlene will show you out."

I breathe a sigh of relief. It seems the Mistresses are almost done making cuts. I so badly want to lower my arms, but I want to serve a powerful Mistress even more. The will to serve is giving me superhuman strength.

"And you," Mistress Insomnia shouts to a tanned young man at the end of the line, "Your fingernails look like you've chewed them all off. Simply unacceptable. Get out."

"Yes, Mistress," the man says, and gulps. I notice one single tear runs down the man's cheek as he and the other reject follow sissy Charlene to the locker room.

"Now boys, take that last one as a good example. He immediately replied correctly and followed my orders without question," Mistress Insomnia says.

"sissy Charlene," she shouts into the megaphone, "Bring the last one back, if he consents to wearing gloves so he can no longer chew his nails. He might just have what it takes after all."

"Yes, Mistress!" Charlene says, and motions the man back into line. Brandon's face lights up with excitement. Had he heard correctly? The Mistress wants him back? Nothing could make him happier. Brandon feels his cock pushing into the chastity cage bars as he becomes aroused at the mere thought of continuing with training. He feels incredibly lucky. The truth is, he'd bitten his nails off because of the stress at his job.

Brandon is 21 and works as a social worker who helps coordinate meals for the hungry in Omaha, Nebraska. His wealthy parents gave him a large lump sum of money when he graduated, and he used it to invest so he could earn passive income while pursuing his dream of social work. He knew he'd probably never break the bank from helping the hungry and was grateful he'd made wise investments with his parent's gift.

Brandon would pay or do anything for the chance to kiss the boot of a true dominant woman. It is something he's dreamed about since he was quite young. In fact, the same woman would come to him in his dreams. She'd be dressed in head-to-toe leather just like Mistress Insomnia. *Come to think of it,* he thinks, *she looked almost exactly like the woman from his dream. Could it possibly have been her?*

Suddenly Brandon's mind is filled with a mental image of Mistress Insomnia holding a leather-gloved finger up to her red lipsticked lips and saying, "Shh…Quiet your thoughts, boy." He shakes his head and looks up at the real Mistress Insomnia. She winks and spanks her riding crop against her leather-clad hands. The Mistresses now face the cohort of New Recruits. I breathe a sigh of relief. I made it through much of the day and the inspection. I am grateful I am still here.

9: Inspiring Speech by Mistresses

"Boys, let me first acknowledge your courage in auditioning for the Arousal Army," Mistress Insomnia announces through her megaphone. She faces the large group of New Recruits, who are set up in a rectangular formation and standing at attention at evenly spaced intervals.

"We know it is not easy to pursue the path of submission in our patriarchal culture," Mistress Intrigue states through her diamond-crusted megaphone.

"Only the bravest can truly submit," Mistress Doom adds. "And quite frankly, not everyone here is going to make it." She thwacks her leather flogger sharply against her palm, and the sound really turns me on.

I return to formation after I finish satisfying my Mistress, but Leonard is still held in the pillory on the stage, and Carl has dozed off in his restraints. I giggle a little because Carl is literally drooling up on stage.

"What was that sound?" Mistress Doom wonders. "You know, boy, submissives are to be seen and not heard!"

Brandon, the social worker, is standing near Quinn, and the two of them are listening intently. Brandon has tried his best to blend in and not rock the boat since he was almost ejected from the whole affair.

"Punish him!" A voice shouts from the row behind Quinn.

"Who is that?" Mistress Doom's head turns on a swivel. She narrows her eyes trying to see who shouted. No one says a word.

The man who shouted is William Stewart. A 37-year-old surgeon, William is more used to giving orders than to taking them.

"It was me, Mistress," William shouts. "Punish that little bitch!"

"Excuse me?" Mistress Doom's voice has a steely cold edge to it. "What part of submissives are to be seen and not heard do you not understand? sissy Charlene, take this one to time out."

"Yes, Mistress!" sissy Charlene replies as she heads across the field to William's yard line. He is the same guy who gave me a hard time about my mismatched clothing when I arrived. *What did this guy have against me?*

I see William watch as sissy Charlene moves, her sheer hot pink tutu bouncing and shifting as she walks. Today sissy Charlene has on white patent leather Mary Jane heels with thick 3-inch heels and a wide strap and button that crosses the top of the foot. sissy Charlene has a slight bounce to her walk that makes William wonders if sissy Charlene is really a man. He certainly does not hold himself like any man William has seen before.

William was raised in Leeds, United Kingdom, by a controlling and verbally abusive father. Although William was drawn to art, his father refused to support his "hobby" and insisted that William go to medical school instead. And young William had learned his place early on. When he spoke back to his father, his dad would give him gruel for dinner and lock him in his room overnight. It felt like a grim fairy tale, but it was routine punishment in William's childhood.

When William got out of his father's home, he studied hard to become a well-paid surgeon. His quest for financial stability was due in part to wanting the independence to be free from his father's abusive words and actions. But while William seems strong and self-assured on the outside, inside he is still a young boy who has been heckled ruthlessly by his own father throughout his childhood.

In fact, the phrase William had shouted— "Punish that little bitch"—is the same phrase his dad said whenever William brought home grades any lower than the top score. And now, just as in high school, William finds himself put in time out.

sissy Charlene grabs William's ear and drags him to a cage made of PVC pipe that sits on the edge of the stage. Inside is a stool and a dunce hat. sissy Charlene unlocks the cage and assists William at getting in.

"Put on the hat and sit on the stool," sissy Charlene directs.

William starts to protest in his British-accented English: "But, I don't think this is necessary."

sissy Charlene cuts him off. "Thanks for reminding me, that's exactly why we have this." She holds up a muzzle with a strap. "Be quiet and let me put this on."

William does not want to wear the muzzle and almost calls sissy Charlene a little bitch, but he holds himself back. He has desired to submit to a powerful woman since he was much younger, and William does not want to blow his chance with not only one, but three, powerful Mistresses. Even though he hates every moment of it, William lets sissy Charlene strap him into the muzzle. Then he sits on the stool and dons the dunce hat. William's cheeks are blushing red as he looks out at the crowd of over 70 half-naked men staring back at him.

"This bell is here for your safety," sissy Charlene mentions. "If you reach the point of no return, where you can no longer stand to sit here and wear the muzzle, you can ring the bell. But please, only use it if you really need it."

"Mmm-mmmf," William mutters.

"Cut the chit-chat. Submissives are to be seen and NOT HEARD!" Mistress Insomnia shouts. Within seconds, William sees her dart in front of his cage and lower her ice blue eyes to his level.

"If you think you'll be successful here by mansplaining and commandeering our event, think again, buddy! We women have lived under this bullshit patriarchy for long enough. That's why we are building this Arousal Army, to help heal the past so we can rise up into our full feminine power and glory and restore balance to the world."

"And that brings me back to the purpose of this speech tonight, gentleman. As Mistress Intrigue points out, the path of the male submissive is not common in our culture. Of every subset of BDSM, male submissives are some of the least celebrated and most misunderstood. But once a domme finds a true submissive, she will love, value, and respect him, and he will open his heart, mind, and soul to her enlivening force. As the two work together, they will both grow stronger through consensual and mutually desired erotic power exchange. With true submission comes true bliss. But all that is wonderful comes with a price, and your path in the Arousal Army will not be easy!"

Mistress Insomnia pauses for a moment and unleashes a new long, thin whip she holds in her leather-gloved hand. I start twitching a bit with nerves when I hear the sound of it whacking against the stage. I can't help but wonder how it would feel if she cracked the whip against my bare skin. I have a bit of a thing for pain. It kind of turns me on.

"In fact, boys, before long, you'll wish all I wanted was your wallet! Instead, I want your total and complete submission. When you submit to me from your heart of pure servitude, I own you—body, mind, heart, and soul," Mistress Insomnia says. She is still wearing her fierce mirrored boots, and she paces across the stage as she speaks.

"The path of a male submissive is not easy," Mistress Intrigue adds. "Just as I had to adjust my expectations and behaviors when I moved to American culture from Japan, so will you men need to adjust your expectations and behaviors as you shed your ego, raised in a patriarchal world filled with unearned male privilege, and adjust to being a simple object that exists solely to serve your powerful Mistress." Even though Mistress Intrigue is no longer a fashion model, she still maintains her slender figure, and she looks like she is posing on stage.

"The luckiest ones will serve all three of us," Mistress Doom adds. "We will choose a select few to be House Ponies. House Ponies get tasks that are less demanding physically, but they must always be well-dressed and exercise the best etiquette and training of the entire stable of submissives. Others will be Work Horses, used for your labor and strength to help develop our private property on the outskirts of Denver."

"You will all be tested in different ways," Mistress Insomnia chimes in. "Though this will be challenging, we want you all to remember, it is also safe, sane, and consensual. If at any point you can no longer tolerate being here, you are completely free to leave. The sissy maids will be more than happy to release you from your chastity cages upon departure."

"And remember what you put in your limits and desires in your contracts," Mistress Doom notes. "What may look atrocious to some may actually be a kink of another, so try not to judge each other's experiences." She pauses and puts her arm around Mistress Insomnia's waist. The two awe-inspiring women stand next to each other and tower over us New Recruits from the stage.

"Each submissive will keep a diary, and you will also receive aftercare in the form of a short touch-base interview at the end of each day or after particularly intense play," Mistress Insomnia says. "But do your best to remain seen and not heard for best results."

"Did you catch that?" Mistress Insomnia stops by Carl, who is still locked in the pillory. She catches herself from slipping as her boot slides into the puddle of drool that has formed beneath his open mouth.

Carl lets out a snore, and his head stays hanging low, with drool dripping out of his mouth.

"Mistress Doom, can you take care of this one?"

"Yes, ma'am." Mistress Doom grabs a cat toy with long dangling feathers. She walks up behind Carl and gently makes the feathers dance across his skin. As the New Recruits watch, Carl's rotund body starts to twitch and move. Before long, he lets out a loud sneeze and opens his eyes.

"Wh—wh—what's going on?" Carl seems surprised to look around and see all the men staring at him. "Oh, jeez, that tickles!" Carl is jumping a bit and moving his body left and right trying to escape the feeling of feathers on his flesh.

"Stand still," Mistress Doom commands.

"Oh, uh, yes, Mistress!" Carl replies, trying to resist reacting to the feathers.

"Good boy," Mistress Doom murmurs as the other Mistresses laugh. Mistress Doom gives him an open-palmed smack on the ass before she walks away. I eye her booty bounce left and right as she moves. "And don't fall back asleep," she adds.

Mistress Doom blows her whistle sharply three times, and the New Recruits quickly run to their primary formation. sissy Charlene also frees William from his muzzle in time out, and he rejoins the group.

Every man makes it to his yard line within 30 seconds—except of course for the ones still stuck in the pillory. I can hear a few whimpers from that direction, and I notice a puddle of unknown liquid—possibly sweat, blood, or urine—has pooled beneath one of the men, a pasty white lump of a man whose face had turned bright red after being held in the pillory all morning.

I hear the click-clack of heels as sissy Charlene approaches the man, presumably to check on his wellbeing. The Mistresses are sadistic and brutal, but they still follow the principle of sane, safe, and consensual. Even though they have cruelly ejected multiple men, they never leave anyone unattended too long or in any really threatening situations. They work us hard, but they want their sissies and Work Ponies to be in good health—physical, emotional, mental, and spiritual.

As if reading my mind, at that moment, Mistress Insomnia steps up to the spotlight on stage and states, "Boys! The finest among you shall one day form the Arousal Army, built to serve the three powerful Mistresses that stand here before you." I jump at the popping sound when she cracks her long, braided bullwhip on the wooden stage.

The beautiful and intimidating Mistress Insomnia is standing on stage on a platform next to Mistress Intrigue and Mistress Doom. They have all changed into thigh-high shiny latex boots with sharp pointed toes and icicle-thin stiletto heels. The boots rise up over the women's leather catsuits. I notice my cock starts to strain in the cage again as I look at the women. I feel my cheeks flush red with embarrassment, and I feel fear I might get ejected if my penis keeps acting up.

I know that edging and orgasmic control would be part of our training if I am selected to serve, and being in chastity for hours each day is already helping us to conquer our lustful impulses and stop being directed by our dicks. I don't want the Mistresses to mistake my excitement for disobedience, as I want nothing more than to serve them. They are so hot! I've never seen any women like this before in real life. They're even more glamorous than the models in *Kinky Times* magazine. Plus, my consciousness is altered simply by being in their presence—and at such a distance! They have such star appeal. *What would it feel like to be in their intimate stable?*

These thoughts are doing nothing to calm my state of arousal. Remembering the telepathic message from Mistress Insomnia from earlier, I try to stop my erection. I direct my thoughts to my finance final exam in college. There had been a very challenging accounting question that was impossible for me to solve. Thinking of the mundane frustration helped reduce the arousal in my chastity cage, though it was difficult to resist responding with arousal to the visual of three hot women in latex and leather before me. I tried not to look at them directly, which they likely preferred anyway.

"We are here to break down each and every one of you New Recruits and build you back up into your true submissive selves, sissy slaves and Work Ponies whose sole purpose and mission in life is to serve us," Mistress Intrigue states with confidence. "You little worms are here to lower yourselves before the glory that is the Divine Feminine Goddess principle and serve us as facets of Her power and grace. Now lower yourselves to the ground in prostration!"

The whip cracks against the stage one more time, sending an electric jolt up my spine. I grow hard, aroused by the snapping sound. All the efforts I made to contain my lust were for naught at this point. I can't help but imagine the bliss of receiving that painful lashing against my bare behind. My cock is sprung hard, and the tip is flushing pink as my man-flesh strains against the metal cage. It is cold and painful, so my erection slowly deflates in its chastity cage.

I throw my body to the ground, hands out front and legs outstretched behind in full prostration to the Triple Goddesses before me. My nude bottom sticks out from the strip of loincloth that barely covers my crack. Other than that and my chastity cage, I am completely naked. I can feel the synthetic Astroturf pressing into my chest and belly. I do not dare look up from the ground, but I glimpse men lying fully flat to both sides of me through the corners of my eyes. I wonder if anyone missed the mark.

"Good job, boys," Mistress Doom shouts through the bejeweled megaphone. "I can tell you have been working hard to learn your signals and formations." I breathe a sigh of relief. It seems I have escaped undue negative attention this round. I hope I am gradually winning myself into the graces of the Mistresses after a rough start. Heck, I figure, women love the bad boy, even powerful Goddesses, right? So maybe each Mistress would see my reckless disobedience as a sort of call to tame me, to shape me, to domesticate me in Her divine image.

A slave that's difficult to train and obstinate can bring a certain sort of pleasure to the right Mistress, I imagine. A brat like me may not be for everyone, but my loyalty and devotion would far exceed the cost of training me. I wonder if Mistress Intrigue might choose me. Rumor is that she is especially sadistic. I feel her eyes on me and hear her voice suddenly echoing from the stage above me.

"We are ready to begin making the final cuts before we sort each of you to your service squad," Mistress Intrigue adds through her megaphone. "Be on your best behavior and work hard to impress us through your submission."

"Yes, Mistress," echoes off the stadium walls as the legions of men shout in response to her command.

"First you will line up in single file, from shortest to tallest. You will have five minutes to sort yourselves out, starting…now!" Mistress Insomnia commands through her sparkly megaphone. She pushes a button on a timer, and I hear the beeps of the countdown begin.

Suddenly, everything is chaos. I see the taller men running toward the back of the line. The shorter guys seem to be avoiding claiming the front spot. There are a few dudes who look to be just around five feet. I see one guy with a thick red beard jostling for position with another dude who looks kind of punk with tattoos. The punk dude keeps standing on his tiptoes to seem a little taller, even though it is pretty obvious what he is doing. Eventually the bearded guy shrugs and steps into the first place, and the other man lowers his heels. I can't help but laugh when I see the second in line is actually probably 4′ 11″ or less. I know it's superficial to judge on height, but at this point, I'll take any advantage I can get!

Eventually everyone gets sorted out, and there are about 70 of us guys in line. Seeing us all in single file makes our various attributes more apparent. Some guys are tan and hearty looking. Others are pasty and pale. Some have huge bellies (like me), and others look emaciated. Some are muscular and strong, whereas others seem weak and lack any bulk. There are old men with wrinkled brows and young men who look barely over 18. And of course, although every man has been caged in a chastity device and fitted in a leather loincloth, I know we each offer a completely different size package. I can't help but wonder, *is bigger better? What exactly do these Mistresses want?*

My thoughts are interrupted by another whistle from the stage. Mistress Insomnia is center stage, spotlighted. Her latex boots glisten in the overhead lights. Behind her, the sun is going down, and the sky is filled with hot pink and burnt orange. I notice the fatigue I feel in my body and hope we will be able to sleep soon. I've made it through the day, but it has not been easy. My stomach rumbles loudly. I haven't had anything but water since my dog food lunch.

As if she has read my thoughts, Mistress Insomnia adds, "You will be sent to dinner after we complete the tribute and boot licking. One by one, step onto the stage, then kneel before each Mistress. Offer your tribute at her boots, and be sure it is marked with your yard line and name. Lick the boots of each goddess you see before you, then exit the stage. Do not take up too much of our time. Understand?"

"Yes, Mistress," the New Recruits bellow obediently from our single file line.

10: Boot Licking

I am in the middle of the line, so I'm not too short, and not too tall. I have my tribute inside three velvet bags. I included $50,000 in cryptocurrency investments for each Mistress, as well as $50,000 in a traditional stock portfolio. In addition, I placed a 1-ounce gold bar in each bag, along with a white gold ring in a jewelry box. Each Mistress will receive a ring that includes her birthstone surrounded by diamonds. I researched them and their interests after I received the acceptance letter.

I also added a special touch to each tribute bag so that each Mistress receives a personalized treat. I know Mistress Insomnia loves floggers, so I am gifting her a leather flogger that is wired to provide electric stimulation. Of course, I secretly hope she might use it on me one day! Mistress Doom is a total stoner, so I give her five pre-rolled joints covered in kief. And Mistress Intrigue, as a former model, loves silk lingerie and hosiery, so I gift her a set of fine silk lingerie and hosiery from Paris, France. I also include a photo of me along with a personalized plea to each

Mistress. I hope that I might be one of the lucky ones chosen to serve all three, so I went all out!

I kind of zone out as I watch 30 or so semi-nude men of various shapes, sizes, and ages bend down, lick the vinyl boots, and subserviently offer tribute to each Mistress. The offerings vary in size and shape. Some are flashy, and some are humbler. Every individual has a tribute for each Mistress.

sissy Rita, sissy Gloria, and some others I recognize from earlier have joined us. They are all wearing matching plaid schoolgirl skirts and sexy white button-up tops with heels. *Were they just doing some sort of role play scenario?* I wonder. *Maybe that's where they've been all day.* I still am not completely sure how things work around here, but I've noticed sissy Rita and sissy Gloria's absence today.

The sissies gather the gifts and place them on a large table on the back of the stage. By my turn, it looks like the Mistresses are having a giant wedding or something, based on the number and size of gifts on the table.

Some men have given cheesy Easter-style baskets filled with luxury goodies and spa treats. Others give small paper-sized packages that I imagine are filled with credit lines, property deeds, or stock portfolios. One showy surfer dude insists on placing the jewelry he brought directly on the Mistresses himself, and sissy Charlene kicks him out.

"But I just want to see these beautiful diamonds on them!" I hear the man squealing as sissy Charlene drags him out. It is comical to see sissy Charlene towering over the loin-cloth clad man. sissy Charlene looks amazingly elegant in her tall heels as she drags the dude toward the locker room.

"Your wants don't matter here," sissy Charlene says snidely. "Did you listen at all today?"

"This is absurd!" The man yells. "I've paid hundreds of thousands to be here."

"It is absurd you'd behave so poorly after you paid so much for complete submission," sissy Charlene notes. "Place the responsibility for this where it belongs—on your overbearing, demanding, mansplaining entitled male attitude!"

"Well, I— " the man interjects.

"The more you say, the more obvious it is that you are a terrible fit for these ladies," sissy Charlene says. She reaches down between the man's legs and deftly unlocks the cage with one hand. She's clearly done this before. "Out! Now!" sissy Charlene shouts.

"But those are really expensive necklaces," the man yells.

"This isn't a brothel. Your money won't buy you access to these women, and they're already so rich, your jewelry does not impress them as much as you think it does," sissy Charlene adds. "These women want someone who is rich with the pure devotional heart of submission. You are not fit to be one of the world's finest submissives trained by these powerful dominatrixes. So I say, good day!"

"Well, can't I at least get the jewelry back?" the insubordinate man pleads. He looks like he is either about to scream, cry, or shit his loincloth. I want to avoid his fate now more than ever. I vow to be completely subordinate and to do my best to overcome my own entitled toxic masculinity. I know individuals of any gender can be abusive, but I don't deny that masculinity has been particularly toxic in modern history.

My women's studies courses had shown me that patriarchal laws and standards have denied women rights that men take for granted for centuries. I am humble enough to acknowledge my own male privilege, even if I am a bit ignorant on what to do to improve the situation. In some way, I hope that offering my complete submission might balance the scales a bit.

I learned about goddess worship and read theories of ancient matriarchies that honored wise women when I took a women's history class at NYU. So, I know some folks think women once were more honored than they are now, and in a weird way, I hope I can help atone for the sins of history by sacrificing myself in service to these powerful women.

sissy Charlene gently nudges the man into the locker room and lets the door slam shut. I imagine that the other sissy inside will take care of the rest. sissy Charlene grabs a walkie talkie and says, "Red alert. Security is needed for Femdom Boot Camp. Please come to the locker room now."

"10-4. Be there soon," a deep voice says at the other end.

I take a full breath and try to calm my nerves. My turn is coming up. What exactly is the best way to lick a boot? I try to stop thinking about germs. Some of the men have gone all out, licking the shiny vinyl boot from tip to top. Others slobbered all over the boots like dogs. I notice a few cocks pulsing against their cages as the men make their tributes. Apparently, gifting is an act of submission that turns them on.

I am glad at least that I feel financially capable of pleasing the Mistresses. My successful hedge fund can rake in a few million per day, so money is no object. And I have a capable team that will be able to run the fund in my stead. As part of my contract, I've negotiated the ability to check in once a week to direct business investments. The Mistresses allowed it, but noted my check-in phone call might be denied as punishment in some circumstances.

I hope my finances, as well as my honest desire to submit, will compensate for my lusty will, addiction to work and alcohol, and previous disobedience. I also made sure my tribute will be big enough to compensate for my lack of physique. Well, it isn't that I am not in shape… it's just that my shape is round. I know I shouldn't be so harsh on myself, but I feel old, ugly, and insecure around these buff, young men—many of whom are probably actually my age or older.

My sedentary, high-stress office lifestyle is not doing me any favors. The daily commute to New York City is taking its toll, and the urban landscape grates on my nerves. It is beautiful out here in the mountains. Something inside me starts to yearn for an even bigger change than I'd originally planned…

"Next!" Mistress Doom shouts through the megaphone. I exit my reverie and look up. The stairs to the stage are right in front of me, and it is my turn to offer tribute. I breathe in deep, then straighten my spine and try to beef up my rather unimpressive muscles. I hold the three velvet bags on a gold tray before me. I try to walk as I imagine they would want a prime sissy to walk, with mincing small steps, as if I were in towering stiletto heels.

I try to emanate humility and servitude as I approach the women respectfully. I've watched enough femdom porn and paid enough attention at Femdom Boot Camp to know that I absolutely should not look the women directly in the eye. Instead, I humbly lower my gaze and try to look impressive by flexing my muscles as I walk toward the powerful women.

I swear I can feel their forcefield from 10 feet away. I slowly and surely walk up each step, counting them to try to calm my nerves. With slightly shaking steps, I mount the stairs, 1, 2, 3, 4, 5, 6, 7, 8, 9—I hold my breath for a moment—10. I have arrived on the same level as the Mistresses.

The stage looks totally different than before, when I was being punished, and when I was pleasuring the Mistresses. Fully masked and anonymous gimps have been rearranging the stage after every major event. Some wear leather masks with dog muzzles. Others have full face masks with eye holes only. They all have mouths with zippers—except one, who dons a full-face mask made of leather with an open mouth, as if he is perpetually giving a blowjob.

Each of them wears the same leather and chain harness getup. They have adjustable leather suspenders united by a leather strap with metal ring clasp. Each suspender has several metal O-rings that can be clipped into the various bondage devices and contraptions the Mistresses prefer. Instead of loincloths, these submissives wear pleated leather kilts that features a tool and utility belt.

I wonder if these are the Work Horses that Mistress Doom mentioned. The faceless men definitely have been working hard, but largely have remained silent. Occasionally Mistress Doom lashes her whip across one of their bare legs or backs to encourage them to work more quickly.

The group of gimps marches out between sets and carries all the furniture and accessories—the gilded thrones, pillories, and so forth—on and off stage. They vanish into an athletic trainer's building when they aren't working and pretty much remain out of sight. At night, these gimps accompany the Mistresses back to the mansion, and I remember seeing a few when I had arrived at the property last night.

But now, I am here. The moment of truth has arrived. Would these Mistresses accept me, my tribute, and my full and complete servitude? Or would I be rejected due to my slovenly behavior and appearance? I feel my mouth twitch nervously, but I keep my eyes cast down and step forward cautiously. I try to play it cool.

The three women together are so powerful that I immediately enter subspace once I am within 5 feet of them. My mind becomes delightfully clear, and I am fully present and focused. I feel so relieved knowing what to do and not having to make any more decisions. If this is a taste of what is to come, I know I am in for a treat. This bliss of submission is exactly what I crave. Now, more than ever, I know I've made the right choice. *Why had I answered that ad? For the experience of total ego eradication.*

sissy Charlene takes my velvet bags and places them in the appropriate places for each Mistress on the gift table. I try to suck in my beer belly to make my best impression on the intimidating and beautiful Mistresses.

I pause as I near Mistress Doom's platform. The busty woman is standing, and her black vinyl boots glisten under the bright stage lights. I immediately drop to my knees and wait for her command.

"Begin the bootlicking now, you filthy slut," she says sharply. Without hesitation I stick my tongue out and lick her boot from bottom to top. I feel my cock grow harder when I near the gap between the boot and the top of the thigh, where I can see the shape of her strong thigh in the leather catsuit. I feel like she can probably snap my head off between her powerful thighs if she wants to.

Mistress Doom never misses an opportunity to offer verbal humiliation. She often calls the New Recruits demeaning names like slut, slave, or bitch. She shows absolutely no remorse and sometimes laughs cruelly as our cheeks blush in embarrassment. She also enjoys making our butt cheeks blush, as Mistress Doom is quick to punish, and quite rough with it, too. It is clear why she works with the less-refined Work Horses in the hopes that they may be good enough one day to become elite House Ponies.

I continue licking her boots up and down until she spanks my ass with a riding crop and says, "You may stop now and move on."

"Yes, M-m-Mistress," I stammer before I crawl across the floor, head fully lowered, to kneel at the feet of Mistress Intrigue. The sadistic Mistress waits what seems like an eternity to tell me to start. After a while, my mind starts to twist and turn, wondering if I should start without her command, or if I'd somehow missed it, or if I was doing something wrong. The longer she waits, the more worries fill my mind. It is psychological torture. Just when I am about to say something—which probably would have infuriated the Mistresses—Mistress Intrigue speaks softly, "Now, you pathetic sack of dog food, you may begin worshipping my boots."

I am so relieved I did not make the mistake of talking out of turn, and I leap at the opportunity to worship her fully. After a quick, "Yes, Mistress," I start the boot licking. I try not to think about the germs of all the other New Recruits who have gone before me. This time, I go from side to side, forming meandering paths along her boots with my tongue. After a while of this, I feel her flogger lash against my upper back. I pause and stand frozen still. "Next," she says, and indicates for me to move on.

I scamper forward still on my knees to the final Mistress, Mistress Insomnia. I feel the most nervous around her because she has a powerful energy field, and whenever I am around her, I can barely put two thoughts together. Plus, I am afraid she can read my mind.

You should be, comes a thought that sounds like it is her voice, along with a vivid mental image of her winking. I almost look up to see if she is truly winking but remember just in time it would be disrespectful for a submissive slave to look a Mistress in the eye.

This world is so different from the realm of Wall Street finance! I feel completely thrown off by the different standards and norms of behavior. Wall Street is still largely a man's world, and I have never felt as unimportant in my career as I have in the past few days at Femdom Boot Camp.

In some ways, this leaves me feeling extremely vulnerable. Without my job title or social status to impress them, do I have anything to offer these women? I want their domination more than I can even express, and I almost cry in frustration not knowing whether I will be accepted into a final squad.

And, it might sound weird, but even after two days of running and marching around in a loincloth with these other men, I still feel extremely self-conscious about my appearance. At least I managed to school that young boy Oliver in how to pleasure a woman orally. That has to have earned me some bonus points.

"Worship my boots, you loser," Mistress Insomnia orders, bringing me out of my thoughts.

"Yes, Mistress," I say immediately.

Lick my boots as well as you licked pussy today, another thought from Mistress Insomnia arises in my mind. This thought encourages me. She noticed my skills? Inspired, I eagerly lick her boots up and down, left and right, and even the sole. I swear I licked a piece of gravel that was stuck in the bottom, but I just swallowed it instead of drawing attention to myself. After I made a few full rounds, she simply says, "Stop now and exit the stage."

I am disappointed she didn't flog me or spank me or offer me any punishment. She probably knows that would upset me. It seems she wants to keep me on my toes. I try not to let it show.

"Yes, Mistress," I say, then crawl to the stairs on the opposite side of the stage. I scamper down on hands and knees, 10-9-8-7-6-5-4-3-2-1, then crawl all the way back to my original spot. I figure I might as well go all out in my complete submission to try to sway them in my favor.

After my turn, I watch Quinn go. He seems to get through OK, without too much event. I wonder what he brought for tribute. Oliver, the young man, is very tall and thin, and stands near the end of the line. The Mistresses make him curl up into a very small ball and bend his head down even further than most of us. It seems like they are trying to physically reduce his size so that they can also psychologically reduce his size.

By now I am starting to recognize a lot of the men, and I know the names of a few that I've spoken to during our down time. Most of the men who have been with me in the limo from the airport made it through the gauntlet just fine, but not everyone survives the process.

Mistress Intrigue dramatically calls for the ejection of a kind of shifty-looking guy with a 5 'o-clock shadow, whom sissy Charlene promptly and efficiently removes near the end. The ill-kempt man offers a respectable tribute, but forgets to say "Yes, Mistress," to Mistress Intrigue after she commands him to lick her boots.

As soon as she experiences displeasure, Mistress Intrigue simply snaps her fingers, and sissy Charlene walks the unfortunate man off the stage. I heard him protesting and begging for another chance, then the slam of the locker room door, and another walkie talkie call to stadium security.

Finally, the tallest man goes on stage and offers his tribute. Each Mistress smiles as he licks her boots thoroughly and sucks on the stiletto heel. He is extremely muscular and has a nice face. I immediately dislike him and—part of me hates to admit it—I want him out.

11: Public Funishment

After the handsome tall man finishes his final act of devotion, Mistress Insomnia stands and grabs her megaphone. The man crawls subserviently off stage and joins the rest of us back on the field on his assigned yard line. I recognize the man as Billy Button, the attractive physical trainer I met in the locker room.

"Boys, look around you," Mistress Insomnia commands. "You will see that only the strongest and most submissive survive here at Femdom Boot Camp."

I look to the left and right and notice that what had once been a line of men that spanned across the entire field is now filled with gaps and holes from those who have been rejected. There are still a substantial number of us remaining—*a few too many,* I think jealously. I still am not sure how I will stack up.

There have been a few more behavioral issues and some disobedience from the other men, but I have definitely received the most negative attention so far of the men who still remain. Most of the others who have failed the Mistresses have been summarily ejected without a second thought. I catch Quinn's eye, and he winks at me, as if to say that we are in this together. I feel my cock pulling again in its cage and blush. *What the heck actually happened last night?* I think. I really wish I could remember.

At that moment, Mistress Intrigue brandishes a long whip and shouts into her sparkling megaphone: "Worms, turn around immediately, bend over, and touch your toes." Caught off guard by the command, I feel myself hesitate, but only briefly. The training is beginning to become a part of me. One instant later, Mistress Intrigue pops the whip hard against the stage and shouts, "NOW!"

As fast as I can, I turn away from the stage and bend forward, attempting to touch my toes. *Damn, how did my hamstrings get so tight?* I wonder. *Must be all those workouts you're not doing,* cackles Mistress Insomnia's voice in my head. I am starting to feel a bit dissociated, almost as if I were hallucinating on drugs. I know what that was like because I tried quite a few party drugs and psychedelics as part of my college fraternity.

Maybe submission is a drug, I think. *This process is breaking down my sense of self, in a weird way that I can't explain. I hope I can talk to Quinn about this later.* I am glad to have a familiar friend in this environment, even though at first, I had been embarrassed to reveal my secret self to him. After all, he knows me as the high-rolling financier from my life back in New York City. But after only two days at Femdom Boot Camp, that life feels like a distant fantasy, almost as if it had been fake. *In some ways,* I think, *it was.*

"Please, have mercy!" I hear a man wail from further down the line. I am not bold enough to raise my head to see what is going on. The man's voice grows frail as he yelps loudly. I hear the sound grow distant, and then I hear sissy Charlene on the walkie-talkies again. Someone else has been removed for bad behavior.

Still, emotionally, I am numb, but that is nothing new. Back home I try to disguise my ennui with sexual trysts and booze. Here the demanding regimen has so far distracted me from my true feelings. Mentally, I am completely exhausted. I want nothing more than to eat a tasty (non-pet-food) dinner and go to bed.

The sun is now setting behind the Mistresses on stage, and the night is growing dark and cold. I feel chills on the skin on my calves, thighs, and bellies. The long line of loincloth-clad men remains bent over. I am starting to feel a bit sore after stretching for this much time.

"Get ready to show us what you've got, boys," I hear Mistress Doom say in her lilting voice through the megaphone. Several pairs of stiletto boots click-clack on the stage, and I imagine the three Mistresses are dismounting the platform. All of a sudden, I hear a loud smack, and the man at the far end of the field yelps loudly, then mumbles, "I am so sorry, Mistress. Please forgive me!"

"Submissives are to be seen and not heard!" growls Mistress Doom. "Yes, Mistress," the man lightly whimpers. I still dare not move my head or look to see what is going on. The smack did not sound like a whip or flogger, so I surmise Mistress Doom is using a wooden paddle on the New Recruits.

The thumping sounds continue, one after the other, and each man takes his spanking in silence. Then all of a sudden, whack! I jump into the air and try not to cry out after I receive my blow. *Damn, that stings!* I think. Mistress Doom is extremely strong physically. Her biceps bulge as she smacks each bare booty using her wooden paddle. She has pommeled dozens of men and hasn't so much as broken a sweat. No wonder she manages the Work Horses!

My ass cheeks burn and tingle, but I still push my butt high in the air, hoping to impress her with my submission. After a minute, I feel the blood flow return to my skin after the initial shock. I imagine my pasty white derriere is flushed bright pink or red, but I can't turn around to look.

Thump! Smack! Whack! I hear the sound of Mistress Doom continuing down the line. The spankings form a staccato rhythm and make a steady beat, until, all of a sudden, the sounds stop. Mistress Doom pauses for what feels like an eternity. I continue to hold my pose and try to follow my breath to quell my anxiety as I'd been taught in mindfulness meditation.

What is happening? Why has she stopped? Thoughts race through my mind. The uncertainty is driving me mad! And my body is physically exhausted. My hamstrings strain as I continue to press my ass high in the air. The leather loincloth flaps over my crack, and my caged cock—*your little clitty!* The voice of Mistress Insomnia interrupts my thoughts. I dare not look toward her on the stage, but I yearn to see her face and form. I want nothing more than to be able to look her directly in the eyes, but I know that would most certainly never be allowed.

Still, I try to have faith. After all, the Mistresses must see something in me, or they would have kicked me out by now. I hope they are impressed by my cunnilingus skills earlier. My—*little clitty*—started to push and pull at its cage. The thought replaces my normal inner dialogue. *What on earth is happening?* I wonder. On top of the weird telepathic stuff, my legs are shaking from holding the forward bend. My stomach is growling, and I have to pee. Femdom Boot Camp is excruciating!

Soon, I hear a high-pitched voice crying out and begging, "Please, beautiful Mistress, please punish me with your paddle. Mistress Doom, I beg of you!" The next man in line must have been unable to handle the wait any longer. The stadium becomes so quiet you can hear the men's chastity cages clanking between their legs. Every New Recruit seems to be holding his breath, waiting to see how Mistress Doom will respond. I can only see Astroturf below me and the men bent over to the right and left of me through the corner of my eye, so I just focus on holding my position.

A few moments later, the smacking sound resumes. Mistress Doom methodically works her way down the row of remaining men. Pat! Smack! Bam! The wooden paddle rebounds rhythmically off the bare behinds. I hold my position, legs shaking, through the end. I hear Mistress Doom shout through the megaphone, "All right, New Recruits! You may turn around and get in line."

"Yes, Mistress!" I shout, along with the others, and return to the lineup. One man is missing... I turn my head slightly to try to spot him out of the corner of my eye, and I notice a hole in the field a few yard lines down. The field has automated trap doors! I imagine the Mistresses have simply pressed a button, and the insubordinate New Recruit was silently and secretly removed from the field. Duly noted—I will not beg for punishment. I can only assume he's been debriefed and removed from the competition.

Honestly, I am relieved. I am tired of trying to compete with so many sexy and capable men. If one more goes home, it is no skin off my back! I renew my desire to pursue complete submission and amp myself up with some confident thoughts. Maybe I have a chance after all.

I turn my eyes back to the front of the stage and hope no one has noticed my wandering eyes. The three Mistresses have returned to the main stage.

Mistress Doom grabs her bejeweled, sparkling megaphone and directs the men to close up the gaps in the line. "Remember, maggots, we will not hesitate to eject you, just like all the other failures who used to fill these spots," she cackles a bit as she broadcasts this message to the New Recruits.

"Put a little pep in your step, slave," Mistress Intrigue intones as she stomps down the stage's steps and onto the field. She charges after Brandon, the man who was almost ejected earlier, and snaps her bullwhip sharply against his bare right cheek. Brandon has an average build and is quite tall, but he has been lagging in response to the Mistress's commands.

I hear the whiz of the tapered tip of the bullwhip as it shoots through the air, then a loud "pop" as it collides with Brandon's rear end. His eyebrows raise up in shock, and he leaps into the air, then scurries quickly to close up the gaps in the line.

"Yes, Mistress," Brandon states, somewhat quietly. I take in his mid-length black hair and caramel-colored eyes and check out his package flopping around, caged underneath his loincloth, as he runs toward me and the rest of the men, who have formed a tighter line.

The 21-year-old squeezes next to me on the right, and Fred is next to me on the left. I don't have time to say hi, but I feel calmed in Fred's strong presence. The older man emanates a sort of wisdom that comes only with age. I watch my anxious, grasping thoughts and lusty actions and feel I might never mature to the level that Fred has attained by age 69. But, I feel less at ease since Fred is ripped and so much older than me. Heck, I can be superficial sometimes, especially when I know I'm being judged harshly by three hot and powerful Mistresses!

I vow to work out and take extra care of my hygiene moving forward. I want to go above and beyond to win my way into their good graces, and one day become their true submissive slave. Plus, I'll be honest, I want to try some freaky shit and wonder what kind of sexual scenarios I might get into with these powerful ladies! Just as my mind starts to wander into a visual fantasy of a foursome between me and the three women, a command from the stage brings me back to the present moment.

"Turn around and bend over now," Mistress Insomnia cries into her bejeweled megaphone. I pivot and bend forward with a quick, "Yes, Mistress." I hear the other men echo the phrase almost in unison. The two other goddesses dismount the stage and join Mistress Intrigue, who is still standing by with her bullwhip in front of the line of men. sissy Charlene flanks the Mistresses and observes the proceedings as the trio moves up and down the line of protruding heinies.

I try to count the number of remaining men and figure it is around 50 or 60, but I can only estimate based on the number of pairs of feet I see out of the corners of my eye. I have held my spot without moving once since I assumed prime spanking position. I've watched the Mistresses set up their submissives throughout the day, so I think I know the exact angle and stance they prefer.

"Ready for your public funishment, you fools?" Mistress Intrigue shouts and snaps her whip against the Astroturf field. I feel the hair on my arms stand up on end.

"Y-y-yes, Mistress," the men respond in near unison. We all sound slightly nervous, and also pretty worn out, though we try to hide it in perky tones. I have to admit all this obedience is getting a bit old. *Am I really cut out for a full-time lifestyle of submission? I want true surrender to the divine feminine, but can I offer the ultimate sacrifice? This morning had been rough on me, and this is just the beginning. Do I have what it takes to survive and thrive in the Femdom Universe?* Doubts filled my mind.

All of a sudden, I hear a loud "thwap" and a nasally voice says, "More, please, Mistress Doom!"

"You don't tell me what to do," I can hear her holler sharply at the man.

"Ouch!" he yells. "That's my ear!"

Mistress Doom has grabbed his earlobe and is pulling him to the Time Out cage on the corner of the stage.

"Submissives are to be seen and not heard," she recites. "And so, you must be punished. Get in the cage and stay there until we decide to release you."

I wonder if the man would consent or resist.

"Yes, Mistress," I hear him say, meekly. The metal cage door squeaks as it closes, and the lock makes a loud clunk as it pops shut. I suppose he has consented, and quickly. That is probably wise. I decide to say, "Thank you, Mistress," instead of begging for more. Clearly the Mistresses did not like that.

I imagine the view from their perspectives: dozens of men of all shapes, ages, and skin tones, bent over, fully submissive, with their rear ends pointed up in the air. I am sure we have flat booties, muscular butts, juicy asses, and thick behinds in our midst.

My booty is a bit on the flat side due to my mainly sedentary lifestyle. Ever since I had moved to New Jersey and started commuting to New York to work on Wall Street, I thought my ass had started to look like a deflated balloon.

I suddenly realize I don't miss my normal lifestyle one bit. Although I crave some creature comforts—a warm meal, a nice shower, some pajamas, and a hug—I do not crave a day in the office. I set up my practice with a trustworthy friend and colleague, and will continue to receive dividends and other passive income from my sizeable investment portfolio while I was at the Femdom Boot Camp.

Part of me wonders if I would end up doing this for life. I want to be humiliated and used by these Mistresses so badly! I stick my flat ass up in the air and try to be patient. I can hear several more thumps as the Mistresses move down the line, spanking each man's bared behind.

I hear Quinn say, "Thank you, Mistress," and Mistress Doom thumps him once more and says, "Good boy." I am happy to know my buddy is doing well and relieved to know expressing gratitude would be well-received. I know submissives are to be seen and not heard here, so it is a risk to vocalize anything at all. I feel I will do whatever it takes to earn my way into the inner circle of submissive slaves.

After a few more "thwacks," it is my turn to be spanked hard. I am nervous with anticipation, and I feel my cock begin to press against the cold steel cage as it grows hard with arousal. I try to calm my lustful desires and focus on pleasing Mistress Doom with my subservience. I press my ass up high and hope she likes what she sees.

With no warning, I feel a solid thump on my rear end. "Ouch!" I shout, without being able to stop myself. "I mean, thank you, Mistress!"

She laughs, and I can hear a hint of her Southern accent. "Here you go, boy," she says, and spanks me again hard with the wooden paddle.

"Thank you, Mistress," I say humbly.

And just like that, she moves on. I let out a sigh of relief. Both Quinn and I have managed to make it through the day's trials.

The rhythmic sound of spankings continues down the line of men to my right. A few men say thank you. Others are silent. Mistress Doom has so much strength and stamina. I marvel that she keeps going with strong swings even when she has spanked over 30 men.

Things go smoothly until the very last man... When Mistress Doom spanks him, I hear him freak out. "I can't take this anymore," he shouts with an unnerving, high-pitched animalistic shriek. I risk a glance to the side so I can see him. His face is bright red, and his fists are clenched. I can practically see steam coming from his ears. Mistress Doom is standing right behind him, still clutching the wooden paddle.

"Bend over, slave," she commands.

"I said, 'I can't take this anymore!'" he shouts, stamps his foot angrily, then turns and punches Mistress Doom hard right in the cheek. Her head reels back at the force of it, and she covers her cheek with her gloved hand.

I hear the click of Mistress Insomnia's heels as she runs off the stage to help Mistress Doom. I can hear her comforting Mistress Doom and rubbing her back, while Mistress Doom tries to hide back some tears. A dark blue bruise is forming right where she was punched.

Mistress Intrigue darts off the stage and quickly uses some advanced bondage knots to restrain the man from further attacks. The slender, tall Mistress is adept in several martial arts, so she easily and quickly overtakes the 230-pound, muscular assailant.

"That behavior is entirely inappropriate in any context, but especially at our Femdom Boot Camp," Mistress Intrigue says. She is standing over the man in her stiletto boots, and he is wrapped in knots and laying prone on the ground.

"Whatever," the man snarls. "You hit me, I hit you. What's the problem?"

"Did you *read* those waivers you signed?" sissy

Charlene shouts, with her hands on her hips. Her face shows her exasperation, and her tutu skirts flutters gently in the wind. Her shiny pink top sparkles in the light.

"You consented to being whipped, spanked, caged, held in bondage, humiliated, and dominated by these women," sissy Charlene states. "Mistress Doom never consented to being punched!"

"Yeah!" Mistress Doom shouts. "When we discipline you, it's for your own good, and it's done with much love and wisdom. You threw that punch from your animalistic, base aggression, and you dare say it's the same as my powerful touch of discipline? That was physical assault!"

"But I can't take it anymore!" The man shouts back. "I'm tired and hangry! Breakfast was shit, I missed lunch because I was being held in stocks on stage—"

"Due to your insubordination," Mistress Intrigue chimes in. "Remember how you talked back to me? Why don't you try some personal responsibility?"

By now, I am feeling quite awkward bent over. I wish the Mistresses would release us, but now they are distracted by this fool. Doesn't he understand how to treat and serve a woman? I roll my eyes at his macho attitude.

Mistress Insomnia clears her throat, "Plus, you have all been trained in the green-yellow-red signaling process, and you know how to activate your safe words. You could have used a safe word or simply used yellow or red to indicate your discomfort."

"Yes, Mistress. I'm sorry, Mistress," the chastened man wails. I imagine he is trying to get back into her good graces by saying that.

I hear Mistress Insomnia snap, and then sissy Rita's heels clicking as she descends the stairs from the stage to the field. I glance over and see she is carrying real iron handcuffs—and not the modern kind, the medieval kind. Her beautiful face, though well made-up, is contorted into a scowl. She lets out a sigh and clamps the cuffs over the rope bondage. Thick iron chains hang down from rings attached to the right and left cuffs clamped tightly on the wrists.

I had tried to gift my ex-girlfriend some novelty fur-lined handcuffs for Valentine's day one year, and she scoffed at them and shoved the gift awkwardly under her bed. She never pulled them out or used them ever again—at least, not while she was with me! I imagined they gathered dust under her bed, but perhaps she let her inner minx out with another partner after me...

I never once got to wrap the handcuffs around her wrists, and I was sorely disappointed. The truth is, I am a switch, and I wanted her to surrender to me as deeply as I desired to surrender fully to her. But I didn't know how to express my desires back then, and she hadn't been open to them, apparently…

Back at Femdom Boot Camp, the ejected man slumps forward and seems depressed. sissy Charlene slips a gimp mask over his face and helps sissy Rita remove the assailant from the main stadium. The police have been called, and a report of physical assault filed. Some of Mistress Doom's top clients in the area are well-connected, powerful men in the police force and—not surprisingly—they love cop role play! She knows they will support her in pressing assault charges against the man.

I feel terrible that the ladies had to waste their time with such tomfoolery, and feel a bit of relief when I hear the door shut behind me as the man is led off the football field.

Despite the drama, the rest of us obedient New Recruits still stand with heinies in the air, ready for our paddling. I hear Mistress Doom take in a deep breath.

"Are you OK?" Mistress Insomnia asks.

"Yes, thank you," Mistress Doom says.

The air in the stadium feels heavy. A silence hangs like a cloud around the New Recruits, still lined up and bent over on the field. I notice the pungent smell of sweaty armpits and groins, a very masculine blend of aromas wafting from the others who are standing so close to me. We are all super smelly after our day of physical effort.

"At ease, gentlemen," Mistress Intrigue shouts, as Mistress Insomnia blows her whistle. I jump back to standing and feel pain radiate down my lower back and legs. We must've held that position for 30 minutes or more while they dealt with that jerk! I am fuming, but vow to calm my strong emotion and maintain equanimity. My daily meditation practice comes to my aid as I follow my breath and deepen the pull of air into my lungs. I feel a sense of peace within despite the tension rising in my body.

12: The One Who Tries to Come Back

Just as I start to feel some relief, I hear some loud yelling from behind the line of men in the stadium. A deep male voice bellows, "I repent of my ways, Mistresses! Please, take me back! I'll do anything!"

Every New Recruit's head swivels around to see who is speaking. I immediately recognize the older man who passed out earlier. I surmise that he must've recovered his energy and regretted what had happened… But how would the Mistresses respond?

Mistress Doom grabs her megaphone and shouts, "On your knees, slave."

The man immediately falls to his knees. He must've been nervous. He is shaking and breathing heavily as he rests on his knees and humbly lowers his eyes to the ground. Somehow, the man manages to let out a, "Yes, Mistress!"

"I am looking for strong men who can work hard," Mistress Doom says. "You don't have to be young, but Work Horses are expected to do manual labor and must be able to toil outside in any weather condition. After passing out before, how can you prove your strength, slave?"

"I will take your most extreme corporal punishment to prove that I am strong enough to withstand pain," the man says.

"Ha! That would be more reward for a masochist like you than it would be doing anything for me. I don't think you have what it takes to be a Work Horse," Mistress Doom says wisely.

She turns her back and walks away from the man, who is still on his knees. He sits in utter silence, as do the rest of us New Recruits. If I'm being honest, I have to say that I really don't love the idea of more competition, and I hope the dude is rejected quickly.

Mistress Insomnia marches up to the man. She looks quite elegant in her catsuit. By now, the sun has set, and the giant stadium lights shining on her knee-high boots makes them glisten. I immediately become horny noticing her, and my cock hits up against the cold steel cage yet again. Still, my semi-erection doesn't instantly drop as it usually does. In fact, it seems to grow harder.

I am more attracted to Mistress Insomnia than any woman I'd ever met. She is so mysterious and powerful… I start to fantasize about stroking her body through her catsuit, and my cock grows even harder. It is painful to feel the cage confining my erection.

Get over yourself and your little clitty! Mistress Insomnia's voice arises in my mind out of nowhere.

She glances over at me briefly—or is it only my imagination?

I have to admit this is tough—and not just the level of physical activity or submission... I am used to having sex—or at least orgasming through masturbating—every day, and sometimes multiple times a day. How am I supposed to sublimate my strong sexual desire and use that force to serve these women? Seeing them isn't helping. Each one is hot in her own way, and nothing like the meek-mannered girls I'd dated before.

Focus, you little bitch! Mistress Insomnia's voice enters my thoughts again, and this time she sounds pissed. I try to return my attention to my breath and calm my mind. I stop looking at the leather catsuit... try to think about baseball... I feel my dick growing a bit softer.

"House Ponies earn their spot through superior performance, and they provide domestic servitude," Mistress Insomnia says. "Stand up, and go with sissy Charlene. She will take you to the stadium bathroom and provide you with cleaning supplies. You can wear rubber gloves, your loincloth, and nothing else while cleaning. You have 25 minutes to clean it to perfection. Go, now!"

"Yes, Mistress," the man says. He raises himself up and walks over to sissy Charlene, who leads him to the locker room where we had originally been caged.

Mistress Intrigue calls us to attention from the

stage. Our heads pivot so we can take her in.

"I may look like your dream, but I'm your worst nightmare," Mistress Intrigue yells through her diamond-encrusted megaphone. She walks in front of the line of loincloth-clad New Recruits and shouts whichever humiliating phrase comes first to her mind. Mistress Intrigue loves to demean and diminish men, but she has no heart for domination. She is in it solely for the money. Or at least she tells herself that. She does enjoy the thrill of being in control for once.

As a young woman in Tokyo, Mistress Intrigue won a modeling contest that propelled her to worldwide fame. As her star rose in the Japanese market, she was booked to model shows in New York, France, and Italy. But although she was world-renowned for her beauty, she felt exploited by an industry that paid models quite poorly, and she was tired of the sexual harassment that was rampant in the industry.

Plus, she felt pressured to stay skinny and look young, which had led to some unhealthy habits. By age 25, Mistress Intrigue felt old and outmoded. She was constantly stressed from living off of fumes from cigarettes she smoked to suppress her appetite. And inside, she was angry and depressed. She felt that if one more seedy man cat-called her, or tried to grab her without her consent, or insisted she sleep with him for a gig, she would hurt him—badly.

Here, though, the submissives come because some of them find pain pleasurable. They actually want the Mistresses to hurt them using their floggers and spanking devices.

The Mistresses sorted them into groups based on their applications. Mistress Intrigue is in charge of overseeing the men who desire to be humiliated, who find public humiliation to be strangely pleasurable, which is exactly her desire and her specialty. These men form the Humiliation Squad and will be trained primarily by Mistress Intrigue.

"You, the pregnant one," she says to me as she walks by, eyeing my sizeable stomach. She stops and looks me directly in the eye. "You're assigned to Humiliation Squad for basic training. I only have room for one—so your beer belly's got to go."

I notice I am so nervous that I am sweating profusely. I can feel the droplets of sweat dripping from my balls. My penis feels strangely hot because it is heating up the stainless-steel chastity cage. At this point, I am feeling extremely uncomfortable. Still, I know my morning performance onstage surely won me some attention, so I commit to soldiering on. Surely we'd get to eat again soon…

"What should you say?"

"Huh?" I emerge out of my thoughts.

"Yes, Mistress," exclaims a voice from behind the line of men. It is the same feminized sissy maid who had measured and fitted the New Recruits for their cock cages, sissy Charlene. She is now in a frilly maid outfit, and appears to have freshened up her impeccable makeup since the morning. Bright red lipstick stains her mouth, and her cheeks glow with a dusty bronze. She has dark eyeliner and smoky gray eyeshadow with silver highlight cream under her eyebrows.

"Oh, right. Uh, yes, Mistress," I thunder with slightly feigned enthusiasm.

"What was that, boy? I didn't hear you," Mistress Intrigue calls through the megaphone.

"Yes, Mistress!"

"Good boy. Now get in line with the other maggots in Humiliation Squad."

"Yes, Mistress!" I scurry over to the huddle of men that had been chosen by Mistress Intrigue. There are 25 men in total in the squad. I can see Brandon, the social worker who had almost been ejected before, among the squad.

The gorgeous sissy maid moves to the front of the line and stands next to Mistress Insomnia, who curls the fingers of her leather-gloved hand and smiles. "Gather the New Recruits," she says to the sissy maid. "You boys will be trained to be my premium House Ponies. Every girl needs a nice pony to ride." Mistress Insomnia winks and giggles.

sissy Charlene prances down the line and hands some frilly pastel-colored panties to the 25 men.

When sissy Charlene passes Quinn, he hands Quinn a beautiful pair of light blue lace panties with extra frills on the rear. They are dainty but large enough for Quinn to wear. There is a hole over his asshole so that Quinn can be exposed for easy access.

"Are you ready to be used?" sissy Charlene asks Quinn and spanks him on his ruffled bottom.

Quinn clears his throat, jiggles his hips flirtatiously, and winks at sissy Charlene. I notice my own cock—I mean, little clitty—respond with arousal when I notice the exchange. *What might that mean…?* I wrack my head to find the memory of what had transpired between Quinn and I last night, but it was ephemeral.

And why is my inner dialogue now starting to call my male pride and joy my little clitty? It seems Mistress Insomnia may be influencing my thoughts... Is she a High Priestess, telepathic, into mesmerism, or animal magnetism? I'd read about some arcane topics in my philosophical inquiries during college…

I glance at Quinn's dark, curly blonde hair kept slightly long, chiseled jaw, and piercing green eyes. He has a ripped chest and a muscular stomach. The man clearly pumps iron. It is a bit comical seeing him here and remembering our other life back in New York as fraternity brothers... I never would have guessed the two of us would be bruised and bloodied after being used and abused by three powerful Mistresses here at Mile High Stadium in Denver, Colorado... What might be next on our BDSM journey? I shiver with anticipation and blush a bit wondering about our future.

sissy Charlene shouts, "Quinn, do you work out so much to compensate for that wee little something barely poking out from between your legs? I measured all of you maggots, and Quinn is definitely the one with the smallest and most pathetic little clitty!"

Quinn's cheeks flush with a blush of pink, and I notice he looks a bit crestfallen. I don't think it is true, either. *I'd seen some guys with much smaller dicks than Quinn, but maybe they'd gotten kicked out? My own cock is smaller than Quinn's,* I think. *Maybe the sissies are just going for some psychological manipulation.* I fathom I am in for plenty of the same since I am sorted with Humiliation Squad. I wonder how I will handle it.

I've always been a bit of a shining star since I have done well in school and been athletic, sociable, and attractive. My success on Wall Street and worldly riches built my ego as well. But now the tables are turned. I clearly need these ladies more than they need me. They care nothing about my titles and accolades. All that they want is my total and complete obedience. What I hope to receive in return is access to the deeply fulfilling experience of subspace, as well as plenty of erotic adventures, and even personal growth and development through facing challenges.

I hear the click of stiletto heels as sissy Charlene prances around on the stage. He announces loudly: "And for those who are wondering, yes, Mistress Insomnia does allow me to test out the New Recruits. So, get ready." sissy Charlene licks her lips, probably imagining the fun she can have with us, and continues to walk down the field at Mile High Stadium. The skirt of her maid's outfit waves in the breeze as she walks, and I can make out her toned ass peeking out from underneath as the skirt lifts up. sissy Charlene is tall and broad-chested, but she has slim hips and strong, muscular legs. She looks like she bicycles because her thighs are huge and strong!

Quinn joins the large mass of men in Humiliation Squad. They are all standing around in their loincloths. Many of them are covered in sweat, and some have scratches and blood on their bodies after the punishments they received during the day's tasks.

One man still has the imprint on his ass of the cat of nine tales that Mistress Doom pulled out during a punishment frenzy on stage that took place during the morning before I arrived. I wince at the memory of being crammed into the wire dog cage, unsure of when I would be relieved. But even though the waiting had been miserable, the entire time, I felt fully confident that someone would return for me. The Femdom Boot Camp has built up a solid reputation for excellence over its 10-year run.

In my time here, I have seen that these Mistresses are ethical and practice the principles of sane, safe, and consensual. I've witnessed them being strict, but they always keep the human's dignity in mind, no matter how harsh their punishments are. I know my fundamental needs and rights will be respected, even if I were summarily ejected with next to no warning. And if I leave—I hate to even let the thought cross my mind. Where would I go then? I crave submission so badly and I've already paid such a high price to be here... The more I experience, the more I want to surrender fully to the three women who embody the divine feminine principle before me.

I return to the present moment. The man with the cat-o-nine-tails imprint is standing in front of me, and I am in awe at how his light brown butt is still peppered with nine bright red sting marks from the flogging implement. Mistress Doom must have wielded it without restraint...

I imagine the man bent over in the stocks on stage, his ass in the air and cock fully caged, with legions more writhing and moaning as they are punished beside him by Mistress Intrigue and behind him by Mistress Insomnia. Perhaps I am trying to assuage my guilty conscience by pretending that someone else has fucked up worse than me. I feel a momentary sense of shame and hang my head. At the moment, I feel like I am only still here because I am really good at giving a lady oral pleasure.

"Put on the panties now, boys," Mistress Insomnia instructs sharply and directly. I can't quite place her British accent. I traveled a fair amount around the United Kingdom one summer during college, but her accent doesn't sound quite the same as the others I heard on my trip. Her words bring me back from my daydream.

"Yes, Mistress," shouts sissy Charlene. A few of the New Recruits quickly join in.

"What did you say?" she asks.

"Yes, Mistress!"

"Good boys," Mistress Insomnia says. "The finest among you will one day experience total power exchange, as I will shape and groom you into the finest and prettiest House Ponies around! Still, the most noble of tasks lies with Mistress Doom and the Work Horses."

"That's right, boys," Mistress Doom shouts into her megaphone. "The rest of you are Work Horses who will be on service squad with me. Expect to get your hands—and perhaps some other things—dirty."

She winks as the men shout on cue, "Yes, Mistress." In just two days, the dominatrixes had turned a group of entitled strangers into a cohesive cadre of obedient New Recruits in their Arousal Army.

"Service squad has got it going on. Good boys," she

says. "My servants love obedience and take pride in their work! We've got lots of strong arms, backs, butts, and legs to objectify as well. I can't wait to make you my property, maggots!

Mistress Doom laughs quietly. I marvel at the contrast between the sound of her gentle Southern accent and the sharp snap she makes with the bullwhip on the stage. I've heard of Southern hospitality and wonder what hers might be like…

13: sissy Charlene's Observations

At just that moment, the older man who was sent to clean the bathroom returns with sissy Charlene. sissy Charlene approaches Mistress Insomnia, who has returned to her throne on the stage. sissy Charlene is donning long white gloves and holds them up to show the Mistress. "This man cleaned to near-perfection," sissy Charlene says. "As you see, there is absolutely no dirt on my gloves."

"By your estimation, does this slug deserve a spot with the House Ponies?" Mistress Insomnia asks.

"I believe he may have some potential," sissy Charlene says. "And after all, he wasn't rejected due to insubordination, but rather, due to physical limitations. He has been perfectly submissive, so long as he has been conscious."

Mistress Intrigue giggles from her gilded throne.

"All right then," Mistress Insomnia says, "This little bitch gets a second chance, and he will be one of my House Ponies."

"Thank you, Mistress!" The man has tears streaming from his eyes. He is still wearing the rubber cleaning gloves with his loincloth, and he has fallen to his knees on the Astroturf. I blink my eyes… Am I hallucinating? I swore I caan see his cock—caged in a mechanism much larger than mine—hanging out under the 12-inch-long loincloth flap. The dude is hung! *So that is why they let him back in…* I think, somewhat bitterly.

What? Are you jealous? You'll never be as big as him. I'd be better served by a dildo than your little clitty, the now strangely familiar voice of Mistress Insomnia speaks in my thoughts. *Get real—your cock makes my pinky finger look huge!*

I hear the sharp snap of the whip on the stage floor.

"Get in line in that open spot now," Mistress Insomnia commands through her megaphone.

"Yes, Mistress!" The man jumps into the spot that is open a few yard lines down from me. I notice some jealousy and insecurity rise up within me. That reject loser should never have gotten a spot. I figure even if he has a giant dick, he is too old to get it up…

This is not my finest moment, I'll admit. All compassion has left me, and I am feeling like a toddler about to throw a tantrum. I am stuck with Mistress Intrigue and I barely made it through the whole day after my morning in the dog cage. This guy gets to be with **my** domme (at least that's how I am starting to see her) after dropping like a fly during our physical activity? I am pissed and a bit scared I won't get a shot to connect with Mistress Insomnia. *What the hell is Humiliation Squad, anyway?* I think.

You'll find out soon enough... cackles Mistress Insomnia in my mind.

The three gorgeous Mistresses all resume their positions at center stage. The gorgeous Mistress Intrigue towers over the others. She's enhanced her incredible natural height with 5-inch stiletto boots, which are made of shiny latex. I note the sexy seam running up the back of the knee-high boots. Her glamorous boots have sharp points, and I catch a peek of the red soles underneath the shoe's arch. Mistress Intrigue has pulled her long hair back in a sharp ponytail, and she holds a black leather riding crop in her hands. Her full-body leather catsuit shows off her tiny titties and bubble butt. I start to squirm, feeling the need to masturbate and relieve my sexual arousal. I can't wait to be free of this cage!

The real cage is inside your heart and mind, my silly slave... Mistress Insomnia's voice floats through my mind. I bring my attention back to the stage. Mistress

Insomnia commands attention from the middle of the group. She wears a leather catsuit that fits her like a glove. She is brandishing a medium-sized leather flogger that she absent-mindedly taps across her hands as she waits for the New Recruits to give their full attention. Her dark hair is cut at a sharp angle, and she has thick bangs that highlight her beautiful ice blue eyes.

Mistress Doom completes the trio. She is the most petite and curvaceous of the three. I guess she is around 5'3," though she appears taller due to her 4-inch fierce, shiny patent leather stiletto boots. As I stare at her ample breasts and curvy body, I feel my cock rub against my cage for the umpteenth time this day. I clearly have no mastery of my arousal or erection. In fact, it is clear my sexual desire is controlling me—all day long, all night long, 24/7.

I remember learning about the concept of hungry ghosts in my Eastern Philosophy class. In Buddhism, these hungry ghosts are caught in a cycle of suffering. They crave endlessly, but have small mouths and will never be able to satisfy their desires. I feel like a hungry ghost, caught in the cycle of *samsara* and illusion…

My stomach growls. It is well past dinner time, and all I've eaten today is a bowl of dog food. That has to have been hours ago. We've done marches, formations, and further training since then. Plus, I held that stress position forever in the final lineup. I am pretty sure the ladies are going to give us the final speech and send us back to the Femdom Mansion compound. I also have to pee.

We have been given a few bathroom breaks during the day, but they were timed, and we were encouraged not to dawdle. I hope I never had to shit during one of these brutal days, and wonder how everyone else is faring. The dog food is not sitting completely well in my stomach. I have a dull pain rising up between my belly and chest. I am not sure if it was indigestion, heartburn, or some type of ulcer... I feel like I needed some Tums, or at least to sit down. My thoughts swirl, and my mind fills with anxiety… I try to breathe slowly and calm myself down. My legs are shaking, and I am sweating profusely. I don't think I can take much more.

"Worms, maggots, and losers," Mistress Intrigue calls through her megaphone and paces back and forth across the stage. Her heels make a click-click-click sound as she walks that is oddly soothing. "The time has come to return to the Femdom Mansion. You have all worked hard today, and so I want to acknowledge you for the gift of your obedient service. Everyone will have a real American dinner—or our equally delicious vegan alternative—tonight back at the ranch!"

I am not sure if I am allowed to cheer, but I sure feel like shouting with joy. A few men say, "Yes, Mistress," but most remain silent. My stomach rumbles again.

"You can all change back into street clothes in the locker room, and the sissies will help remove your cages for the night," Mistress Doom directs.

"Then, join your travel groups at the limousines, which will be waiting out front," Mistress Insomnia adds. "Dinner will be served as soon as we return, so dress like the gentlemen we know you are."

Mistress Doom blows a loud whistle and says, "New Recruits, you have survived! And you are officially released to the locker room."

"Yes, Mistress," I say, with the other New Recruits.

I feel overwhelmed with gratitude as I begin walking to the locker room. A hand taps my shoulder, and I turn around. I feel good when I see Quinn's familiar face smiling at me. He swats me on my ass and winks.

"Are you ready to get out of this cage?" he asks.

"Hell, yeah," I say. "I've wanted to jerk off about a million times today."

"I've heard rumors that the Mistresses are going to clamp down on our freedom to orgasm," Quinn says, "so you might want to get your release while you still can. Let me know if you need a hand." He chuckles and looks down, smiling.

I blush. "Well, what did you think of today?" I try to change the subject.

"I have never been worked so hard in my life," Quinn says, "and I was on the NYU basketball team! The basketball coaches were tough, but they're nothing compared to these chicks."

I look around to see if anyone was listening. I have a sinking feeling that the Mistresses would not like being compared to baby birds.

That's what the ball gags are for, Mistress Insomnia states matter-of-factly in my mind. Am I really hearing her, or am I going crazy?

"Quinn, I think I've been having telepathic messages from one of the Mistresses," I say.

"What? You're tripping after too much physical

activity," Quinn laughs. "Telepathy isn't real."

We reach the locker room and stream in with the rest of the men. I glance around and see quite a few men who look almost broken. Femdom Boot Camp is not for the faint of heart… But that damn good-looking Billy Button comes running into the locker room, chest and abs glistening from sweat, with a huge smile on his face. He jogs to his locker and starts pulling out his street clothes.

How on earth does the dude have that much energy? I wonder. The familiar feminine voice fills my thoughts again: *He's energetic because he didn't eat dog food for lunch due to his insubordination, among other reasons…*

I swear Mistress Insomnia is sending me psychic messages, directly through my thoughts. It also seems she can read my thoughts, which is quite unnerving. I shake my head to clear my mind, then unlock my locker and pull out my black slacks, leather belt, and a gray Calvin Klein T-shirt. I grab my red silk boxers as well. Though expensive, they feel so amazing against my skin! Still, I haven't brought a suit jacket to the stadium, so I plan to freshen up my hair to give myself a bit more of a gentlemanly appeal.

I hear the click of heels approach me. It is sissy Phyllis, who is wearing a bright purple head-to-toe fishnet body stocking, along with a bright pink tutu. I can see that the sissy is caged in chastity as well. sissy Phyllis has a dayglo yellow wig on and colorful makeup that rivals that of any drag queen. The beautiful sissy is wearing hot pink latex boots and bright pink lipstick and nails to match. "I'm here to remove your cage," sissy Phyllis tells me.

sissy Phyllis pulls a key from a clump of keychains and squats down in front of me. I am still bare-chested and my big gut hangs gently over the top of my suede loincloth. sissy Phyllis pulls the flap aside and quickly inserts a key into my cage. With a deft touch, she removes the cage, and I sigh with relief. I am tired of feeling the cold metal against my semi-erection, and I am done with having my penis restrained.

Reading about male chastity and actually attempting it are completely different things! I am happy to have a break for the night, and I hope I will adjust to my new situation quickly. I still am not totally sure I am cut out for a life of 24/7 submission, but I definitely am not willing to give up this chance to try!

"The driver is waiting out front to transport you to the compound," sissy Phyllis tells me. I breathe a sigh of relief and wave to Quinn as I walk toward the exit. It feels good to have my normal clothes on, and I am especially grateful the physical exercises seem to be done for the day. I haven't run as much in the last five years as I did today while practicing formations! My body is completely exhausted.

My physical tiredness doesn't stop my mind from generating anxious thoughts, though. I still feel guilty for drawing the ire of the Mistresses this morning, and I wonder if I have managed to enter back into their good graces. I suppose I am still here, at least, so there is that. At this point, I've seen over 30 men ejected, and so I know I am lucky I haven't been sent home yet.

The limo is waiting out front, and I join the now-somewhat-familiar crew inside the car. The group seems to have a lot less energy than we had when we first landed at the airport, but we also feel more relaxed around each other after watching each other run around half-naked all day.

"You sure do clean up nice, Theodore," Kahua calls out.

"Hopefully you stay out of the dog house," Leonard snickers. "I've never seen a grown man in a dog cage like that. That was hilarious!"

"Ha, ha, so funny!" I say, while rolling my eyes. "I'm not going to remind you about the time you fell right in front of Mistress Doom, and she simply said, 'Ew,' and literally walked on top of you in her stiletto boots, like you were simply a rug. Oh wait. I just did."

"You know what, guys? Today's been hard enough without us turning on each other," the young Oliver states. I think he is being a bit naive. I've been in Wall Street long enough to know it is definitely human nature to backstab, exploit, and manipulate. I am slightly suspicious of the other men. After all, it is a bit of a competition for the affection and attention of the three Mistresses.

"Oliver's right," Andrew says. "I'm a lover, not a fighter, and I'm here to have a good time."

"Yeah! Plus, our ranks are growing thinner," Fred says. "Thomas was kicked out of Femdom Boot Camp. That's almost one-tenth of our group that left after just one day! Who knows how long the rest of us will last?" Carl issues no comment, as he has dozed off in the corner of the limo and is snoring slightly.

At that moment, Brandon opens the door and manages to get his 5'11" frame into the limo by hunching down. He is the last remaining member of our group, so the chauffeur pulls away from the stadium and begins driving to the Femdom Mansion compound at the outskirts of the city.

I close my eyes and try to complete a moment of meditation during the drive. I feel my mind still and my thoughts grow calm as I follow my in-breath and out-breath. After about five moments, I open my eyes and see that Brandon has joined me in meditation. I close my eyes again and dive deeper into my own consciousness.

While I feel the car moving, my mind deepens and clears. I feel my body relax, and I begin to notice my emotional state. Guilt, fear, sadness, and anger shoot up seemingly from nowhere. Apparently, this process has generated more frustration within me than I've realized.

Truly, my challenging emotions make sense. In everyday life, I am master of my domain, but here, everything I've known is being subverted. The thrill of it is both arousing and frightening, all at the same time. I have to admit I love the feeling of giving up control. It is beginning to fill me with a special sensation that I can't get any other way, and I find myself craving more sweet submission.

After a while, I feel the car stop, and I open my eyes. Brandon opens his as well and smiles at me. "Were you meditating?" he asks.

"Yes," I say. "Were you?"

"Yes," he responds. "It really helps me stay strong and clear-headed in my social work career."

"What kind of social work do you do?

"I help individuals suffering from food insecurity in my community in Omaha, Nebraska," Brandon says.

"That's great, but how can you afford to be here?" I ask.

"I'm an investor on the side," Brandon says. "I got into cryptocurrency early, and my small investment has really supported me in living my dreams. I was able to use that to finance my entry fee."

"Wow!" I say. "I work in finance also, but I'm a traditional hedge fund manager on Wall Street." I notice saying those words feels weird to me now, a bit hollow. I am beginning to feel more like a New Recruit than a financier. Something inside me is changing, and I am not quite sure if I like it or not…

Brandon opens the car door, and the rest of us file out and enter the mansion. I don't see any gimps this time, but occasionally I hear some loud cries coming from a room nearby. It sounds like a sharp male shrieking sound, and it is difficult to tell whether he is screaming in ecstatic pleasure or ecstatic pain. I wonder what is going on…and if I'll ever find out what is in the other rooms!

sissy Charlene appears and begins directing us to the ballroom that has been filled with our cots. "New Recruits, go sit on your cot and wait for everyone to return."

"Yes, sissy," the group replies. The cot is labeled with my yard line number, so it is easy to find. When I get to my cot, I am pleased to see that my luggage is still placed right next to my bed. I sit and watch the other New Recruits continue to swarm into the ballroom. A few have red marks or bruises from punishments they received earlier in the day. We all look quite different in our everyday clothes as well.

A loud bell rings out over some sort of intercom system, and an unfamiliar voice intones, "New Recruits, dinner is now served in the informal dining hall. Proceed to dinner now. You may take bathroom breaks as needed for the rest of the night, but no New Recruits will be able to leave the house. The doors are locked and alarmed, and there are surveillance cameras outside the building. Trust me, the Mistresses will notice if any of you worms sneaks out!"

The voice monotonously continues, "Remember,

you are not held in chastity now, but that does not mean you have full reign to do as you please. Continue to abstain from indulging your primal lusts even when uncaged, gentlemen. Here, even the walls have eyes and ears, so be on your best behavior."

That last line makes me a little nervous. I already feel like Mistress Insomnia is somehow receiving and responding to my thoughts. Plus, it is obvious the sissies will be monitoring our behavior, but how else might we be observed while we are here? I try to recall what had been in the fine print of the waiver I signed, but I had been so excited to get here that I hadn't paid too much attention to the finer points of the contract.

I sneak a glance at Quinn, who is sitting on his cot on the opposite side of the room. Now that his physique is fully covered up by his street clothes, I realize I miss seeing him almost nude in the loincloth. There has been a strong sort of sexual tension between us, or at least I feel there is one…

I still can't completely remember, but I have to wonder if it has anything to do with what happened last night? I vow to investigate matters further when I get a moment alone with Quinn. He meets my eye and smiles. I feel my heart leap a little bit. I still can't believe I've run into my former fraternity brother from

NYU here in Denver at Femdom Boot Camp.

The high-ceilinged room features around 100 cots oriented into rows that fill the extravagant luxury ballroom. The threadbare canvas military cots contrast with the opulence of our surroundings. The walls feature elaborate molding, the wallpaper has gilded French Rococo designs, and the polished hardwood floor beneath the metal legs of our cots has an elaborate parquet design. It seems the Mistresses enjoy gold, white, and black. The mansion incorporates these elements into the design of each room. The ceilings on the ground level are high and lofty.

I glance up and see a Michelangelo-type painting that fills the ceiling of the ballroom. It is painted in a classical style like the painting from the top of the Sistine Chapel, but instead of featuring scenes from the Old Testament story of the creation of the world, the mural features erotic scenes of female domination.

In one panel, latex-clad dominatrixes tower over naked male slaves, who are wearing full gimp masks and who are featured sitting on their knees on the floor, eyes lowered. Another one shows a plump nude male slave who is strapped to a bondage cross. His eyes are wide, and he has a ball gag in his mouth. His tiny cock is held in a chastity cage. Mistress Intrigue is painted standing behind him and holding some rope. The final panel shows a Femdom Boot Camp scene, with dozens of loincloth-clad men in rows and the Mistresses on stage.

"They've been doing this for a decade now," Fred, who has the cot next to mine, tells me when he sees me ogling the art. "I heard some of the sissies were at the original Boot Camp 10 years ago." He chuckles, and I feel myself drawn to the guy. He seems super genuine and kind. I want to know more about Fred's story. He is pushing 70, so he has to have had some pretty interesting experiences on his path that led him here. I bet the world has changed a lot since he entered it in the 1950s…

"That's amazing," I say. "What brought you to Femdom Boot Camp?"

"Well, this might sound weird," Fred says, "but I think it is a spiritual calling. I mean, sure, technically I saw the ad and answered it, but something about it feels divinely inspired. I grew up in the Bible Belt in Alabama, and I still feel that connection to the Holy Spirit and God that I used to feel in church as a child. But my mind's expanded a bit, and I want to push myself further."

Fred continues, "I've lived a lot of life. I left the South to pursue my dream of being a pro basketball player when I was recruited by the Chicago Bulls after college. Being a star player was fun, but I still want more. I want something only a strong, powerful woman can supply, and so that's why I'm here."

So that is why Fred is so tall and athletic! He is a former pro basketball player. "Now that you mention it, I might have seen you play!" I tell him.

He smiles and stretches his arms up overhead. "Who were you in your former life?" he asks.

"Well, I was a hedge fund manager on Wall Street," I say. "I mean, technically I still am; I left the fund running with my partners in my absence."

"So, you're a money guy then," Fred smiles.

"Something like that," I say.

A series of loud beeps comes through the overhead intercom system. "Dinner is served. New Recruits, line up in order of your yard lines, and sissy Charlene will lead you to the cafeteria," the anonymous voice states. The other New Recruits and I stand up and begin sorting ourselves into a line. I notice about 1/3 of the cots are empty and surmise that many men have been sent home today. I wonder how many of us will be left by the end of Femdom Boot Camp.

I file into line and follow the New Recruits in front of me. I can barely make out sissy Charlene since she stands several inches taller than even the tallest New Recruit in her heels. The scent of hamburgers and hot dogs fills my nose. This American cooking smells so much better than my dog food breakfast. My stomach rumbles.

The buffet lines are staffed by shirtless men wearing only chef's hats, tight leather pants, and collars. I grab a tray and make my way through the buffet. I end up with an authentic American meal: a burger, fries, and a chocolate milkshake. I navigate to Quinn's table and sit near him. No one else is nearby.

"Hey, buddy," he says and winks. He picks up the hot dog and takes a bite. I can't help but notice he looks hot with the sausage in his mouth, and I briefly imagine him pleasuring me, then blush.

"Hey man," I laugh, a bit nervously. "What'd you think of today?"

"Never seen anything like it," Quinn says. "Honestly, I'm glad I survived this ordeal! And I'm glad you made it through, too. What was it like this morning getting punished?"

"Honestly, it was tough," I say. "It's better to obey than go through that, that's for sure!"

Quinn scoots close to me and whispers in my ear, "Want to unwind like we did last night?"

"About that..." I pause and sigh. "I can't believe this, but... I don't remember last night. What happened?

At just that moment, sissy Charlene enters the dining hall with sissy Phyllis and sissy Rita. They form a group at the front of the eating area. The large room, which has been filled with the murmurs of conversation, is suddenly silent. Every New Recruit stops what he is doing to listen to the sissies, who are dressed impeccably, as always.

sissy Rita blows a whistle, then announces, "While you were enjoying your meals, we conducted a search for contraband."

My stomach drops. I should've known something was up. This meal is too easy, too delicious, too normal.

"You might remember the house rules: no booze, no pornography, and no drugs—unless you brought some marijuana to gift to Mistress Doom."

This is not going to be good for me, I think. sissy Phyllis continues, "The following New Recruits have been found to be in possession of contraband and will need to be punished. When I call your number, step up to the front of the room."

I suddenly notice sissy Rita carries a long chain like an old-fashioned chain gang might wear. There are several ankle cuffs all joined together by a longer metal chain. The chain features connected arm cuffs and even a metal collar for each person. Today sissy Rita is wearing a form-fitting silver sequined gown with flashy glitter heels.

One by one, sissy Rita calls numbers, and New Recruits jog to the front of the room with heads hanging low. sissy Rita locks them into the ankle cuffs and then puts each one in a gimp hood. I can feel my heart rate speeding up. There is one set of ankle cuffs left.

"47N," sissy Rita shouts. I gulp, glance again at Quinn, then trudge to the front of the room. In a bid to being obedient, I stick my ankles out to be chained. I figure it will be easiest not to resist arrest. I get one last look at Quinn's gorgeous eyes, and then the world becomes darker as the gimp hood is pulled over my head.

"The rest of you can go back to your room and

enjoy a night of leisure," sissy Phyllis states. "You might enjoy perusing our extensive library of femdom erotica and feminist literature."

"And you naughty boys, you can come right with me," sissy Rita says and laughs maniacally.

This does not sound good. I feel the chain gang start to move, and I try to keep pace. The ankle chain is surprisingly heavy, and after a long day of physical exertion, I feel myself dragging behind. All of a sudden, I feel a sharp pinch on my ear and let out a yell: "Ouch!"

The pinch grows sharper, and then I feel the sting of a leather riding crop on my behind. I leap in the air and scurry forward. I am glad I at least have clothes on to block the blow. *Not for much longer...* Mistress Insomnia's face fills my thoughts. *Get ready for some special punishment time with me.* I can hear her cackling in my thoughts. *I may look like a dream, but I'm your worst nightmare...* I can't help but wonder one more time, *why on earth did I answer that ad?*

"Gentleman, your punishment awaits..." sissy Charlene says, and ushers us into a cool, dark room. I can see almost nothing through my gimp mask, but I feel the weight of the fetters around my ankles. I can smell the sweat from the men nearby.

From the shadows, I hear the crack of the long whip against the wooden floorboards.

"Welcome, my slaves," one of the Mistresses says. "Let me do the honors of introducing you to how we do things here in the Femdom Mansion." She cracks the leather whip sharply against the ground again.

"You'll never be the same after your first real punishment. So, let's get on with it. Who wants to go first?" she asks.

"Me," I say, and shuffle forward. I figure it is the only way to possibly earn my way back into good graces.

"Good. Then I will make an example of you," she says coldly. I feel her tug at my arm, and then the lights go out in the room…

TO BE CONTINUED IN BOOK 2:

BONDAGE BOOT CAMP...

About the author

Back matter

Printed in Great Britain
by Amazon

24829135R00159